WHAT WE CALL LOVE

Enjoy!
♡ Esther

WHAT WE CALL LOVE

ESTHER HUESCAS

NEW DEGREE PRESS

WHAT WE CALL LOVE

ISBN 978-1-63676-549-5 *Paperback*
978-1-63676-117-6 *Kindle Ebook*
978-1-63676-119-0 *Ebook*

have you ever felt consumed by love?
have you ever felt yourself grow into the person
you strived to be?
have you ever felt alive in the arms of another?
I urge you to chase the feelings that remind you of the worth
there is in living.
you must remember you are worthy of it all.

- ESTHER HUESCAS

To everyone I have had the privilege to love and to be loved by. To everyone who has believed in me. To everyone who has encouraged me to dream. This book is for you.

CONTENTS

A NOTE FROM THE AUTHOR

Dear Reader,

The most common question people asked me when I initially told them I was writing a book about romance through different perspectives was, "Why?" They may have wondered what qualified me as an expert on the topic. How can I, as a nineteen-year-old Latina, effectively represent all the different demographics my characters embody? These are all valid questions. I asked myself the same ones as I wrote, so allow me to explain.

The problem I saw with most coming-of-age stories is that they don't tend to focus on minority groups. Also, more often than not, the romantic feelings teenagers and young adults feel in these stories are often invalidated due to their age or "immaturity." With my novel, *What We Call Love*, I hope to show you that every love story is unique. Everyone's differences are not only okay, but they are also what make the feelings real.

I have paid attention to my own relationships and to those that surround me. With this book, I have taken the time to reflect on what love truly entails and why we struggle so much to define it.

That is the goal of *What We Call Love* is to show that defining our feelings is a different experience for everyone—for the characters who come from different cultural backgrounds, for myself, and for you, the reader. My characters are from different neighborhoods in Chicago. They have different home lives, stressors, sexualities, and passions. This book journey has taught me what a privilege it is to love someone, regardless of the outcome.

Although this is a work of fiction, I couldn't have written this novel without the inspiration of my past experiences. As an author, I have myself, at times, become stuck, not because I am out of content to write but because I struggle to channel the emotion I am trying to convey onto paper.

My parents' relationship was my first real example of what love meant. I found myself thinking that their example was common until I began comparing their story to those of my friends' parents and those in the media. They both immigrated from different cities in Mexico with little money and dreams of finding success. They met at a fountain in the Division Blue Line stop in Chicago twenty years ago—a love by chance. When I started making these comparisons, I very quickly realized how unconventional their story was. Working long hours left little room to focus on spontaneous romantic gestures. Yet, regardless of the inconsistencies in their unconventional story, I cannot invalidate their feelings. Their relationship later influenced my other experiences.

My middle school relationship taught me that my body's appearance would make me the target of unwarranted sexualized attention, just like many other women. In high school, I saw how all these experiences would affect my life, which taught me how our past can impact the way a relationship grows and how we define it. It's the differences that make the feelings so hard to understand but they are valid, nonetheless. Every romantic moment in my life, especially the failed ones, have taught me to value myself as an individual before anything else. Time heals, and recently I have begun to see the brighter side of what love and relationships hold. I hope this book can teach you to never settle for less and that every story is worth retelling.

I could not have written this novel without my friends. Their stories and advice have influenced these characters and have allowed me to represent more than just the story of a Mexican American woman. I am so proud of the representation of black and brown communities in this novel. It is because of my LGBT+ friends and family that I have been able to include their stories and try my best to represent that community as well. I couldn't have done this without the members of my friend groups and my community in Chicago, who trusted me with the privilege of getting to know their stories through interviews.

Music has also shaped the way I view the journey of finding oneself immensely. Music has an ability to help youth express their complex emotions. It was an enormous influence on me while I wrote this story, so I chose to have a song title at the beginning of each chapter. I encourage everyone to listen to each song at least once.

Additionally, I incorporated my love for poetry into my novel. Each chapter begins with an original poem. My hope is to take you on a full experience when reading *What We Call Love.*

Lastly, the city of Chicago has been a consistent inspiration. In this book, the locations of the most romantic scenes showcase what makes Chicago unique. Some places mentioned are the Montrose Harbor, the Ledge, Lake Shore Drive, Downtown, and some hidden neighborhood gems. Chicago, to me, is a city of romance, opportunity, and hope, especially for the youth.

The true answer to the why behind this story lies in you, the reader. This book is for you if you are from Chicago or any large city where you know it is easy to feel lost at times. This book is for you if you are a minority and have ever felt like you don't belong. This book is for you if you have ever been in love or find yourself waiting for the one. This book is for you.

Love,

Esther Huescas

PART I

I.

MARIPOSA

"Sandstorm" - Mereba ft. JID

starting something new can be suffocating
as it reminds us of all the times we've failed
but the only way to find something better
is by daring to ignore fear
and allow ourselves the chance to experience love.

-ESTHER HUESCAS

JUNE 2019

I laid on Serenity's bed, staring up at her ceiling and waiting for a text from Jayden that I knew would never come.

Serenity ran into her room. She moved my long, black hair to the side so she wouldn't sit on it, then jumped onto the bed beside me. She asked, "Mari, you ready for tonight, girl?"

I pushed Jayden to the back of my mind. I decided I would overthink about him later. I hugged her. "Of course," I said unconvincingly. "We're gonna turn up with you."

Everything for the party was coming along pretty well. I almost never drank; I couldn't handle losing control of my body. We would rarely go out and party in high school. We honestly saved the fun for summer and spent the school year studying as much as we could. We all made a pact to make it out of the hood.

That night though, I made an exception since it was Serenity's eighteenth birthday. Her mother worked night shifts every Friday, so the night before her actual birthday, we all helped her set the party up.

"Okay, perfect. Who knows, maybe you'll find yourself someone cute. Mari, it's time to give one of these boys a chance so we can finally go on some adorable double dates this summer before college."

"Yeah, we'll see. That'd be fun." I looked for a distraction on her shelves filled with poetry and love stories. I knew I wouldn't think of anyone but Jayden at that party, but I hadn't told Serenity about us.

When we realized things wouldn't work out between the two of us, it became easier to pretend our relationship never happened. Honestly, I was embarrassed to tell anyone, even my twin brother Elijah, because I didn't even really know why we didn't work out. I did have a couple of ideas, though.

Serenity grabbed my hand. "Come on, no more hiding, weirdo. Let's go wake up Raymond." Her bedroom led to the hallway that connected all the rooms in her one-floor townhouse in Bronzeville. We made our way to the living room. Before she got to the couch, she went around the room and made sure to close the windows to keep the bugs out while we could. Chicago summer nights always led to a ridiculous amount of mosquito bites.

Serenity paced back and forth and turned to Raymond, who was falling asleep on the couch. He was so tall his legs blocked anyone from walking in front of him.

"Raymond!"

He startled.

"When is Jayden getting here with the drinks? It's been a damn hour since he said he would be here. It's already six!"

She wasn't the type to yell, especially not at her boyfriend, Raymond.

He jumped up from the couch. "Babe, Jayden said he's on his way, so that means he's on his way. Come on now, you know how he be acting. Don't worry, the party ain't even gonna start until ten."

Serenity had always been like this. Everything needed to be perfect and organized; she loved knowing how the story would end. We instantly bonded over our love of literature, and I was her shoulder to cry on when she struggled with her parents' divorce.

After pacing in the living room, Serenity turned to face us. She turned so quickly her long brown braids whipped behind her. "I know y'all both right; it's just I can't help but worry."

After summer break, Serenity was planning on going to Columbia University to study writing. Raymond had taken a gap year to work in the city and was taking classes at the University of Illinois at Chicago. He was waiting to hear back from New York University to study music after being wait-listed. I really hoped he would get in so he and Serenity could take on New York together. Jayden was a year ahead of us like Raymond, and he had been studying medicine at the University of Illinois at Chicago.

Elijah, my twin brother, was planning on going to Northwestern University to study engineering. I was headed to the University of California Los Angeles in the fall. The party was for me Serenity, and Elijah—a goodbye to high school. We would all face a new reality in the fall, away from each other. Even the idea of leaving gave me goosebumps.

Serenity sat back down next to Raymond, and he smiled and softly kissed her forehead. "I love you, but you only gotta worry about having a good time tonight. I'm gonna go grab some last-minute things for you, and I'll be back at eight, okay?"

I loved the way he looked at her. All it took was her being in the same room as him for her to be his entire focus.

"You best not get here late," Serenity said. "I need you next to me before everyone starts coming!" She followed him to her front door.

Raymond shined his pearly white teeth and kissed Serenity before walking out into the late June heat. It was early enough in the summer that when he opened the door, the sun was still fully shining.

"Mari, I want to be done with the decorations and everything by the time Raymond comes back. Do you mind making a cute sign for the glowsticks?"

"Glowsticks? What glowstick sign are you talking about?"

Serenity playfully rolled her eyes. "Girl, didn't I show you the picture of the glowstick party theme I saw online the other day?

I shook my head no.

She sighed, "Okay, so basically there are three colors for the glow sticks; green, yellow, and red. Green means you're single, yellow means it's complicated, and red means you're taken. So, when people walk in, they'll grab the one that fits their relationship status. It's cute, and it'll help there not be any love drama tonight. 'Cause you know how these guys get about their girls."

Serenity was right; there was always that one guy at the party who would hit on the wrong girl with an angry boyfriend. I couldn't help but wonder what color Jayden would pick.

I connected to the speaker on the kitchen counter and Serenity said, "Yo, you better not play too much of that sad shit you listen to."

She always clowned me for my music taste, which I swore was superior. "I have to. Nothing tops my sad song playlist."

Serenity rolled her eyes then giggled. "You know, for someone who won't give anyone the time of day, you sure do listen to hella heartbreak songs. Who got you in your feelings?"

I shook my head. "No one."

I didn't see the point in admitting to Serenity that I wasted my time on a boy who didn't want to commit to me. I also wanted to stay true to the promise Jayden and I made the past summer. We promised each other that we wouldn't say anything to our friends, so the group's dynamic wouldn't change. It had been pretty easy to pretend everything was normal, because Jayden had been busy with college the past few months. Tonight, I knew I had to go back to pretending like I didn't want to kiss him. I hit shuffle and "Lovely" by Brent Faiyaz filled the air.

* * *

MAY 2018

Jayden showed me that song on our accidental first date. We were the only ones free from our friend group that summer night, and since we were all best friends, it wasn't weird to go to the party by ourselves.

I took an Uber and met up with him outside the three-story house that belonged to some rich kid who went to our school. The party was on the north side of the city by Irving Park and Southport. The first two hours we were there, everything was normal. We were drinking, dancing, and talking to some people we knew.

They were playing some remix of a rap song, and the room was completely filled with people dancing the night away. We were standing against the wall for a bit just sipping on our drinks. But I couldn't help but notice from the corner of my eye that Jayden was staring at me for a little too long, so I screamed over the music, "You good?"

"Yeah, you?" he asked as he pulled me closer to him to spin me to the beat.

I couldn't help but laugh at how goofy he was acting. He had the people around us whispering, but I didn't even care. "Yeah, I'm great."

As soon as I said that though, he shook his head disapprovingly and took me to the DJ booth. He opened his notes app and typed *"Lovely" by Brent Faiyaz*, then showed it to the DJ. Thankfully, he was friends with the DJ, so he didn't have to beg too hard.

The song started playing, and we danced to the song as he sang every word by heart facing me. I was so into the song

I didn't even notice how almost everyone had managed to move to the other rooms. They were complaining about the DJ not playing the Top 20 songs on the radio. Jayden, by the end, had me smiling with my entire face.

The fairytale almost ended when the police pulled up.

Shouts of, "It's twelve!" echoed throughout the entire house, and the sounds of panicked drunk teenagers filled the hot summer night air.

I felt a pit in my stomach at the thought of the police, but Jayden didn't hesitate.

He immediately grabbed my hand and ran for the door. I didn't even realize where he was taking me until we got there. We ran all the way to Wrigley Field. His touch gave me butterflies, and in that moment, I swore I felt like I could have done anything.

Surprisingly, we made that ten-minute run without tripping on anything or getting stopped by the Chicago Police. We stopped and sat on the benches in front of Wrigley Field to wait for the Uber we were going to share to go back to our homes.

"Okay, it says ten minutes till the car comes."

"Okay, beautiful." He rested his head on mine.

I didn't think much of his words because him hitting on me was a running joke; one no one ever took seriously. I was convinced it was just him playing around. Part of me was scared to let myself believe it could mean anything more.

We sat for a moment in silence, listening to the people laugh and stumble down the street as they came out from the sports bars.

Jayden lifted his head and turned to face me. He was avoiding my eyes, and I couldn't read him like I usually could. "Mari, I shouldn't be telling you this, but I gotta."

I reached for his hand, and he gave me a soft squeeze back. "Come on now, Jayden, you know you can tell me anything."

"You really are beautiful."

I couldn't help but laugh at how dramatic he was being over a compliment. "Thank you. Why you acting all weird about it?"

He laughed and shook his head softly. "I don't think you get it, Mari. To me, you're perfect."

My dumb ass had finally figured it out. He must have seen me put it together because he pulled me closer, and suddenly, I realized my heart felt like it was about to beat out of my chest. He held my face softly and led his lips to meet mine. It was perfect, and everything was still so innocent.

The kiss was sweet. The feeling of his soft lips pressed against mine lingered long after he pulled away.

The Uber came, and once we got into the car, we didn't say a word about the kiss. But God, was I losing my mind. I didn't know why he kissed me and if it even meant anything to him. Or if it was just the liquor and the adrenaline of running from the cops that got to him.

I couldn't even look him in the eye. I was stuck trying to figure out if the connection had always been there. He didn't even try to mention it the entire ride back, either.

The driver played "Secrets" by The Weeknd, and I turned my focus onto the lyrics to drown out my thoughts.

Once we got to his house, before he got out of the car, he didn't hesitate to hug me goodnight. He had his hand on the door handle when he casually added, "Umm, could I by any chance see you again tomorrow?"

I wondered what he really meant by that. Did he mean a date, or did he mean to hang out again, just as friends? He normally would always text me to hang out, so it was weird for him to have asked in person. But I insisted on seeming carefree. "Yeah, that sounds good," I said without hesitation.

"Text me when you get home. I'll pick you up tomorrow at six."

"I will. See you."

He hugged me goodnight, and I could smell his cologne.

He thanked the driver, and with that, he went into his house. Fifteen minutes later, I texted him that I was home. He loved the message immediately, and then I went to sleep.

I woke up to the smell of my mother's *chilaquiles*. My father was playing *corridos* in the kitchen and singing every note almost perfectly. I was sure that if he had the money and time, my father could have recorded a song and lived out his dreams. But it was hard to dream for something like that because they were undocumented and had to make sure our family had enough food to eat each day. I learned from a young age that the "American Dream" wasn't a reality for everyone. I thanked God that UCLA had given me a full ride. That's why we all worked our asses off through high school to make sure we'd have good enough grades to get full scholarships.

I got ready for the day. I touched my fingers to my lips, remembering my kiss with Jayden the night before, and butterflies grew in my stomach. "*Hola, Mami.* It smells amazing in here."

"*Hola,* Mariposa. Did you have fun at Serenity's house last night, *corazón*?" She didn't wait for me to answer. "I'm sorry I couldn't be here before you fell asleep. I didn't get home until three." My mother served some food on a plate and brought it to where I was sitting.

"Mariposita, I feel like I haven't seen you all week," my father said as he hugged me and kissed my forehead.

"*Papi,* I know, but I heard you singing my favorite *corrido* this morning," I said with my biggest smile. "Serenity and I watched a movie and don't worry, I knocked out as soon as I came home."

My twin brother, Elijah, walked in with his hair ruffled up. He went to kiss both our parents on the cheek. "*Buenos días.* The food smells so good."

"Wow, you slept good, huh?" I asked as I pointed at his dark brown curly hair he hadn't bothered to comb before breakfast.

"Real funny, Mari, like you›re one to talk." He was able to look serious for a second but ended up cracking a smile. Elijah was naturally my best friend, but I didn›t know how to tell him about Jayden without it being weird. So, I chose not to say anything. We had a secret agreement to keep our partying and questionable activities away from our parents.

The television in the kitchen was playing Univision, and they were reporting from the lakefront, the city skyline behind them. "Look at how pretty Chicago looks," I said.

My mother apologized every time she couldn't tell Elijah and I goodnight in person. I would never blame her; she was my hero. My mother, Rosalia Marquez, grew up in a small town in Mexico. She loved everything about her home. "Yes, but Chicago to me will never compare to my *lindo pueblito,*" she said. "The city is too loud, people are too in a hurry, and they are too quick to judge. I have never felt at home here. I tried for my parents, my brothers, for your *papi,* and for you and Elijah, but—" She shook her head in what I thought was defeat.

Elijah and I looked at each other for a while, at a loss for words.

"*Mami,* but now it's our home," I said.

My brother and I hadn't seen our father all week because he worked late into the night and would wake up early to work again. My father, Enrique Marquez, grew up in a small city and crossed the border by himself when he was twenty years old. With tears in his eyes, he said, "Ay, Mariposita, without this beautiful city, I would be nothing. It has given me work, and that has given me every other blessing in my life. It led me to meet your beautiful mother and have you and your *hermano*." He kissed Mami, then looked at me, his stare serious. "And one day, you'll meet a *muchacho bueno*."

I rolled my eyes, but I was grinning too.

He turned to Elijah. "And you, you'll meet a *muchacha buena*."

Elijah looked down, immediately more interested in his plate of food. He shoved a forkful in his mouth. I thought it was weird, but Papi kissed my forehead, interrupting my focus.

We finished our breakfast. Elijah and I hugged our parents goodbye when it was time for them to go to work.

My mother gave us her *bendición*: "*Mariposita y Elijah que Dios los bendiga*. We'll see you guys later tonight."

* * *

JUNE 2019

"Lovely" had ended and "Love" by Kendrick Lamar was playing. I could see why Serenity thought my music taste was so sad, but songs like those brought me peace. Maybe I was a bit obsessed with love—not necessarily with the feeling of it, but with its very existence.

I had only ever told one boy that I loved him: Jayden. It had been months since Jayden and I last talked. Since then, I'd turned eighteen and was left healing from a relationship that hadn't even really started. I was left to dream about the endless possibilities that could have occurred if time ever cared. The problem with endless possibilities is that the chances of happiness and sadness always seem equally possible.

My mess of a situation-ship with Jayden left me wishing life was more like a math problem with proven formulas and theories. I wished that if I followed all the rules, I would get the right outcome every single time. I realized there wasn't a set of rules for love, and even if they existed, people broke them.

I finally finished making the glowstick poster when Serenity came out of her room. "Mari, come help me with the drinks. Jayden just got here. He's got Elijah with him too. I thought you said he had a soccer game, so he wasn't coming till later tonight?"

I was nervous to see Jayden, especially because he continued to flirt with me in order to make sure our friends didn't suspect anything out of the ordinary. I also mentally thanked Elijah for being here, so there would be more distractions. "Elijah? I know damn well he did, and there's no way it got canceled. I don't see any thunder or lightning."

We walked through the living room and opened the door onto the porch, where we were greeted with a gust of hot air.

"Wassup, y'all ready for tonight?" Jayden asked while looking at me up and down with a shy smile. I couldn't help but notice how good he looked with the sun shining on him. He had on a crisp white t-shirt that complemented his brown skin and made his gold cross necklace pop. He had on distressed jeans and some royal blue Jordans. He also knew exactly how to look at me.

I had become really good at pretending to be unbothered. "Jayden, it's been a minute. How you been?" Without waiting for an answer, I turned to face Elijah. "What are you doing out here, dummy? How'd you get done with your soccer game so quickly?"

"Mari, chill. It got canceled. Aren't you happy that I get to turn up earlier with my bestie, Serenity, for her birthday?" Elijah said while hugging Serenity.

"Boy, you lucky I ain't no snitch," I said. Elijah just rolled his eyes and went back to checking his phone. I wondered who had his attention like that and made a mental note to ask about it later.

Serenity laughed. "Y'all stay coming at each other, but yes, bestie, I am glad you made it this early." She then turned to hug Jayden. "Yeah, it's been a couple weeks since we've all been able to hang out. What you been up to?"

"Oh, you know, just trying to get Mariposa to let me take her out," Jayden said, and then winked at me.

I got that he was trying to convince our friends we were still good, but he was blowing me with all the damn compliments. I couldn't help but roll my eyes at him, even if I did want his words to be true. "Jayden, I don't know how many years are gonna pass until you understand. We are never going out like that." I went to hug him to soften the sting. I'm not sure who hurt worse from my words: him or me.

"Jayden, this is just getting sad, for real, man. I›ve been watching my sister curve you the last three years, and you ain't gotten the message yet. She doesn't like your goofy ass." Elijah playfully punched Jayden's arm.

Jayden shook his head. He looked toward the floor for a second, then instantaneously looked up with a smile. "Y'all just don't get it. I'm gonna marry you, Mariposa."

For a split second, I questioned whether he was just saying those things or if he actually meant them. I wouldn't let myself fantasize for long. I rolled my eyes and joined them laughing.

We were really good at pretending that we hadn't said we loved each other the summer before. We were really good at pretending like we hadn't done a lot more than that the summer before. I was convinced we deserved a damn Oscar for our performance because I was still in love with him.

II.

SERENITY

"Can I Get Your Name?" - Katch

you taught me life is filled with uncertainty when you left
nights lost wondering,
did you ever really love me?
days I'll never get back, thinking,
did you ever think I was enough?
people I'll never get to love, as I asked myself,
did you teach them how to hurt me too?
you taught me to doubt myself when you left.

- ESTHER HUESCAS

JUNE 2019

It started to cool down as the sun began to dim into the horizon. I looked down at my watch, and it read 7:36 p.m.

"Jayden, shut up and stop bothering Mari. You know she doesn't want your bum ass," I said.

He would have normally taken my comment jokingly. I was just teasing, yet he seemed to take it to heart this time. "Serenity, not all of us are lucky enough to meet our soulmate when we were fifteen."

"Stop talking about all that, Jayden. You're depressing everybody! Now, let's all get inside and put these drinks in the fridge. I can't be out here giving people warm beer." I pushed them off the porch and into my house. Meanwhile, Mari dragged the wagon full of liquor behind her. Elijah and Jayden ran to the two soft, blue couches in my living room and threw themselves on them as if they had just finished a marathon.

Mari went to the kitchen area to organize the cups and fill up the chip bowls. She set the overflowing wagon next to the fridge.

I caught Jayden looking at Mari again, but he said to me, "Yo, Serenity, where Raymond at? I've been tryna call him, but he isn't picking up."

"He left around seven and said he was getting my surprise for tonight." I was excited to find out what he had planned, but part of me was also worried about why he was being so secretive.

Jayden's eyebrows raised. "You all good?"

I smiled. "Yeah, don't worry about me. We all good." They always said that Raymond and I were the parents of the group. I wondered if they kept secrets from us like kids tend to do.

Mari looked up at me and gave a look that said she knew me better than anyone else. She was the only one who could notice I was lying through my teeth. She left it at that though—just a look—and kept on doing her own thing.

* * *

DECEMBER 2016

Raymond and I met in our math class when I was a sophomore. I know it makes me sound like a hopeless romantic, but I didn't believe in the possibility of falling in love with someone as soon as you met them until I spoke to Raymond for the first time.

When I first saw Raymond at the beginning of the school year, I told Mari that I thought he was cute, but I wasn't spending my time daydreaming about him or anything. I knew there was more to life than crushes. Honestly, up until that point, I was more invested in the romance between the characters in my books than in my real life.

It was a couple of days before winter break when Raymond came up to me in the hallway after class. He tapped my shoulder and instantly smiled when I turned and saw him. "Hey, my name's Raymond. You Serenity, right?

I couldn't stop myself from blushing. "Yeah, I know, and this is my best friend Mariposa."

Mariposa waved. "It's nice to meet you, Raymond. But, Serenity, I gotta run to class. I'll catch up with you guys later."

I thanked her with a smile and continued fidgeting with my backpack strap.

Raymond waited for Mari to leave before laughing. "Remind me to thank her later for getting me a few minutes alone with you."

"Yeah, she's pretty smooth like that," I said while admiring his perfect, short braids and thinking about how cute his laugh was.

"Yeah, I can see that. What grade y'all in? I feel like I haven't seen you before this class. I mean, this school isn't that big. I should've known there was someone as beautiful as you here."

I giggled. "I guess you didn't look hard enough then, 'cause we're sophomores. We been here for a while. How about you? What year you in?"

He started fidgeting with his hands. "Damn, I guess I've been tweaking for a year then. I'm a junior. But, listen, I've been eyeing you for a while now, Serenity, and I would love to get to know you better over a proper date."

It took everything in me not to scream with excitement, but I held myself together. "Yeah, I would like that."

He beamed with joy. "Perfect! Here, lemme get your number and you can send me where you want me to pick you up from. This Friday sound good to you?"

He handed me his phone, and I put in my number. "Yes, sounds perfect." I don't know why, but something about him asking for my number in a time where social media ruled romance seemed like a good sign.

I felt my heart beating fast, and I began to realize that those chocolate-brown eyes and glowing dark brown complexion were going to make it hard not to fall in love. The bell rang, so we quickly said bye and ran to our classes in opposite directions.

I got to class completely out of breath and settled into the empty seat Mari had saved for me next to her. As soon as I could stop smiling like an idiot, I told her that I had a date Friday night.

* * *

LATER THAT WEEK

Friday night came, which also happened to be the last day before winter break. So, even though I was nervous about my date with Raymond, the day kind of flew by. Mari went all the way out to my house in Bronzeville to help me get ready and pick out the perfect outfit. We went straight to my room and started going through my closet.

"Serenity, I think this is it!" Mari said, laughing as she held up the Eeyore onesie I had bought for Halloween two years before.

I laughed with her. "Girl, what you tryna do? Make him cut me off after the first date?"

Mari turned back to my closet. "Okay, lemme stop playing 'cause didn't he say he was getting here at seven? It's already six. This is much more like it." She held up a maroon sweater dress and thigh-high black boots.

I smiled at her. "Yes, now you're acting like the fashion icon I know and love!" I grabbed the dress and boots from her and started to put the outfit on.

"You should wear these small gold hoops with it too. It would look good with the gold cross necklace you always wear."

"You right, you right!" I did love the way the outfit looked. Mari always knew how to style everybody.

I did my makeup, and Mari took countless pictures of me before she left. It was getting late and she had a long train ride from the south side to the northwest side where she lived. She took the long train ride a lot, though. Especially when I was going through my parents' divorce. She stayed by my side through all my ugly cries.

At seven on the dot, the doorbell rang.

I ran to the door, looked through the peephole, and opened it to see Raymond.

He wore a dark blue, almost black, dress shirt. For some odd reason, it made his already perfect eyes pop out even more. He paired it with straight black jeans and a black belt with a thick silver belt buckle. He had on the nicest black dress shoes I had ever seen. He topped the outfit off with a black puffer coat that was honestly just practical considering it was 19 degrees out and snow had begun to fall.

He looked me carefully up and down before focusing on my face, which somehow made me even more nervous.

"Wow, you look beautiful," he said as he pulled out a large bouquet of wine-red roses he had been hiding behind his back. "Here, I brought these for you." His hand slightly shook as he handed them to me.

"Thank you, Raymond. They're beautiful." I had a fascination for roses and flowers in general; there was something poetic about how we cut them as a symbol of admiration and affection, just to have them die in front of us.

I locked my front door and followed Raymond to his black 2016 Toyota Camry. He held the door for me before I got in—a small but sweet gesture. His car smelled of men's cologne, but not in a bad or overpowering way. I would learn to love the scent.

Raymond looked over at me when we reached the first red light. "So, what type of music do you like, beautiful?"

I looked down, embarrassed that his words were making my cheeks burn. "I like old school soul, R&B, and rock, but don't get me wrong—I appreciate new school rap, too. I got a few trap artists in my playlists as my guilty pleasures. What about you? What type of music makes you feel something?"

"So, you an old soul in a young body then? Nah, I mean, I appreciate the greats, but I truly love modern slow R&B. I can feel their sadness for real. But don't worry, we gonna put each other on! You put whatever you want on our way there, and on the way back, I'll share my story through music."

He had the sunroof open and the windows slightly down. I felt the air hit my face. "Okay, I like it. But you haven't told me where we're going, so how am I supposed to tell you my story if I don't know how long I have?"

"That's the point. You got to treat each song like it's the last story you can tell. It's okay if it's incomplete, almost all of us will never be able to finish our stories before we stop being able to tell them."

"Okay," I said and played "Then You Can Tell Me Goodbye" by Bettye Swann. I don't know why it felt so vulnerable to show him songs I actually loved. We listened in silence until the last note. His silence was driving me crazy.

"Okay, so you like the old love songs then?" he finally asked.

His question made me nervous. "I mean, I guess. How can you not love Bettye's voice?" I didn't tell him that the reason why I loved older music is because my father would play it in the car for me when everything was still good.

"Yeah, her voice is beautiful, but what she's singing about is what's important. Don't you think?"

I couldn't help but feel like I could tell him the world. I don't really know why, but I would like to think it was because of how honest he was being. I felt like I could let my guard down. "Yeah, it's the lyrics that stick with me. I feel like the older artists are the only ones not sugarcoating all the aspects of love. The way singers talk about romance today can't compare to how they used to do it."

"I can't wait to prove you wrong. I'mma show you on the way back that some people still know love, but alright. Next story?" He had one hand on the steering wheel and the other resting on the windowsill.

"Yeah," I said while putting on "Let's Stay Together" by Al Green. The song was a beautiful background to watching the city pass us by from Lake Shore Drive. We passed the Buckingham Fountain, and soon the lake stretched as far as my eyes could see.

Again, we sat in silence and listened to Al Green sing about love. This time, the silence didn't make me feel uncomfortable or like we had run out of things to say. It felt peaceful.

When the song ended, he said, "Okay, this is slightly cheating, but you have just enough time for one more song."

I laughed softly and played "Weak" by SWV, this time letting myself sing along to every single word.

He finally pulled into the parking lot of a small Italian restaurant, but we stayed an extra thirty seconds in the car so my last story could finish playing.

"Come on, we can continue this after dinner," he said.

"Yeah, that sounds good." I hadn't realized how tired he looked until that moment. I wanted to ask him about it, but was that something you mention on a first date?

He got out of the car and walked over to the passenger door to open it for me then extended his hand to help me out.

We made our way inside. The hostess greeted us and led us to a corner booth. The air smelled of fresh pizza.

I started looking at the menu but kept getting distracted by all of the holiday decorations. Tiny paper snowflakes hung from the ceiling, and the walls had fresh wreaths. The normal lights were dimmed and fairy lights around the windows lit the seating area.

"Well, you know where I live now and have seen my neighborhood in all its glory. Where do you stay by?" I asked while I wondered whether to get pizza or pasta.

He looked up from his menu. "I live in Uptown. Been there my entire life. It's not the safest but hella white people are moving in, which means they're kicking us Black people out. Gentrification is happening all over the city and attacking the Black and brown communities most."

My eyes lit up as soon as he started to talk. I wondered how he was even real; he loved music, was educated on Black issues, and looked absolutely gorgeous. I responded, "I guess I really only started getting exposed to other cultures at our high school. Before that, all I had known was Black people. You're definitely right though. I mean, I live hella close to the University of Chicago, and every year, the white students try their hardest to take over. I thank God that gentrification is moving slower there than in other neighborhoods."

"Yeah, I don't know what I would do at that school without my friends."

I agreed. I don't know what I would've done without Mariposa by my side. "So, going into high school was a huge culture shock for you, too?"

"Yeah, of course. I mean, it was just weird being in the same learning environment as so many different people. Since we all go there, we're technically all equal, but I'd be lying if I didn't admit that I find myself having to work ten times harder for half the recognition. I guess we gotta get used to it, right? Especially if my parents are gonna force me to go to med school."

Before I could respond, the waitress came and took our orders. I ordered the shrimp alfredo, and Raymond chose a small pepperoni pizza.

As soon as the waitress left, I asked, "So, your parents are forcing you to become a doctor? What's that about?"

"They didn't come to the United States for their child to not be successful. To them, success only comes with being a doctor, engineer, or lawyer."

"Where did they come from?" I asked curiously.

"We're Nigerian," he replied.

I nodded my head. "If you could do anything without your parents telling you otherwise, what would you do?"

"I don't know. I mean, I like sciences. I really do. I just don't feel like I could happily do them for the rest of my life."

"Okay, well let's start with what you like to do for fun."

"I love music! I've been playing instruments ever since I was little. My family taught me how to play the guitar, piano, and drums when I was younger. I sing and play for fun, but it's never been an option in my house to pursue the arts."

"Wait! Hold up, Raymond. You tryna tell me you know how to play all those instruments and sing? And you're barely telling me?"

He started laughing. "Should I have started with that?"

I felt my cheeks burning. "No, I mean I'm just saying it wouldn't hurt for you to try to do something with music. I bet you're great, and I'm sure your parents would understand if they know you love it."

He smiled, almost sadly. "I mean, I have thought about it, but only as a dream, not as something realistic."

I reached across the table for his hand and smiled up at him. "Listen, how about I promise to be your biggest fan no matter what?"

His eyes lit up.

Before I knew it, we had flown through three hours of conversation and had made our way back into the car. It was now his turn to show me his story through music.

"Serenity, I need to see you again. I know our first date is not even over yet, but I just need to let you know that there's gonna be a second date."

I got goosebumps but tried to convince myself it was because of the cold and not a guy making me nervous. I smiled. "Okay. I would love to get to know you more."

We listened to the lyrics of love songs all the way back to my house. When we got there, he parked the car and started getting ready to open my door.

"Wait, don't leave the car yet," I said.

He scooted back in and looked at me attentively. "Yeah, what's up?"

"I don't know." I paused and pushed a strand of my hair behind my ear. When I gained some confidence, I said, "I wanted to thank you for everything tonight." No person—especially not a guy—had ever made me feel more beautiful.

"You seem to know what you want. I hope I'm in your future plans for a long while, Serenity."

I bit my lip. "You're so damn cheesy! I don't mind it, though. I guess I just wasn't expecting it from your demeanor."

He looked slightly offended but quickly seemed to get over it. "What did you expect from me?"

"I mean, honestly, I guess for you to just hit on me and then drop me after you got what you wanted."

He looked slightly more offended by that comment. "What did I do to deserve that assumption?"

"No, nothing." Truthfully, how could I not be scared about that? I didn't go around trusting just anybody. He was attractive and it was so easy to talk to him; I was terrified that I would catch feelings. I had it stuck in my head that chances were high that I was just setting myself up for heartbreak.

I think my silence said what was on my mind better than I ever could, because he said, "I'mma show you that I'm not gonna hurt you. Alright?" He slowly inched closer, his eyes fixated on my lips.

My heart was beating fast, and my palms were sweating. I mentally thanked God that he wasn't holding my hand. "Okay," I whispered before letting the side of my face rest on his cool palm and his soft lips meet mine.

After we pulled away, we just smiled at each other like idiots for a second. Then he helped me out of the car and walked me to my door and met my mother. She didn't even mind that it was after eleven once she got a taste of his charismatic personality.

He flashed a bright white smile at her. "Would it be okay with you if I take Serenity out on another date next Friday?"

My mom grinned back at us both. "As long as Serenity wants to go, I won't get in the way."

* * *

JUNE 2019

I was worried about what we were going to do after the summer ended and I had to leave for New York. Yet, it didn't change the fact that I saw myself married to him one day.

Instead of exposing me, though, Mari said, "Elijah, Jayden, y'all better get up and start helping me put the drinks into the fridge."

Jayden sprung up from the couch and Elijah followed, groaning all the way to the kitchen about having to help Mari.

I loved the way Jayden looked at Mari. I don't know why, but she had never been the type of girl to give anyone the time of day. She's always been the perfect example of the happiness that comes from being single.

My parents' divorce made me appreciate Mari so much more. Because although she didn't personally understand it, she always listened.

My mother used to tell me that when I was born, she and my dad were still arguing about what to name me. My dad suggested "Serenity." My mom told me it was the prettiest name she had ever heard, so she let my father get his way. My father used to tell me he chose Serenity because I was the tranquility that God had sent to bless him. Growing up, I seriously thought their love for me would be enough to keep them together, but it wasn't. Some people just aren't meant to be together, and I've learned to accept that.

It had been four years—my entire time at high school—since I had last seen my dad. I wondered if he would be proud of me for getting into Columbia and for being our class valedictorian.

My father, Jeremiah King, was always the smartest man in the room. Most people just didn't know it. He worked tirelessly to make sure I always had what I wanted. His only priority in life had been me and my mom, at least until the alcohol made him a shell of the man he used to be. My mother, Amara Davis, supported him through his addiction, but he just didn't want to get better.

Things got a lot harder when my father left. My mother became fiscally responsible for both of us because after buying his liquor, my father never had enough money to send child support. Some days, it felt as if he had never left, and other days, it was hard to even picture his face before the addiction took over. Four years is a long time to go without seeing someone. I couldn't help but wonder if he missed me and my mom when he was sober.

* * *

AUGUST 2015

It was a warm August night in Chicago when my mother told me we were leaving my dad in our house in Bronzeville. She let me know we were going to my grandma's house in Englewood.

"Baby, I'm going to need you to get up and go out with me tonight," my mother whispered softly in my ear.

I rolled over to face my alarm clock. It read 12:32 a.m. I whispered back, "Why so late, Mom?" Despite my question, I knew better than to not do immediately as my mom said, so I jumped up from my bed.

"Baby girl, it's important! I already packed your bag. Don't worry about bringing anything but your pillow and blanket," my mother whispered.

I followed my mom out to our car and fell asleep before we had even reached Grandma's house. Most of the next morning was a blur, but I do remember that my mother spent an hour trying to explain to me what their divorce meant for us.

"Serenity, baby, your dad says he loves you and that he wishes he could say goodbye, but he can't be in this city anymore."

Imagine how fucked up that could have left me.

I sat on my grandmother's couch and bawled. I only stopped to hiccup in order not to choke.

When my mother realized I wasn't going to be able to respond, she kissed my forehead. "We're going back home tomorrow, okay? So, sleep today, love."

* * *

JUNE 2019

I didn't like to think about the divorce or my father often anymore, and I was definitely not trying to be thinking about those things the night of my birthday party. Birthdays were always hard, but this eighteenth one meant I was becoming an adult. Some politician had decided that today was the day I no longer legally needed my dad, even though he had decided that for me four years ago when he left.

I knew Raymond would know what to say to snap me out of this funk. Almost as if he could sense my sadness, I got a text from him. It read, "*Babe, you gonna love my gift! Get ready! ;)*"

I replied, "*Super excited, but come to my house. I need you here!*"

"*Don't worry. I'll be there before 9! I'm just handling some business with Jayden with the liquor!*"

Jayden was standing damn near right in front of me and had just asked me where Raymond was. Confused, I asked, "Jayden, you heard from Raymond recently?"

Jayden looked at me strangely as he kept putting the beers in the fridge. "Umm, I just told you like ten minutes ago that I hadn't. But don't worry, I'll let you know if I do."

I stared at Raymond's text for what seemed like an eternity. I didn't know how to reply. What was I supposed to say? He was lying to me and I didn't know why. Honestly, I was scared to know why.

III.

JAYDEN

"Frio" - Omar Apollo

God has a funny way of helping us move on
made the best loves seem like they are by accident
by one single "impulsive" choice
made it that the loves where you still have someone else on your mind going into it
the ones that end up meaning the most
taught us the reason why the other one didn't work out
is because there was someone else better in store.

- ESTHER HUESCAS

JUNE 2019

Serenity walked over to Mari with something clearly on her mind. She whispered something to Mari and immediately started consoling her. Mari looked so beautiful, like always, and I wished things weren't so complicated between us.

From the moment I met Mariposa two years ago in 2017, I knew I wanted to keep her in my life. I almost kissed her then, but our first date wasn't until a year later. She was the only one who knew what my flirty "jokes" meant. I just wished I hadn't fucked up so bad last year.

* * *

JULY 2017

We met at a rich kid's pool party when she was sixteen and I was seventeen. I wasn't even planning on going; I was just chilling at home when Raymond Facetimed me. Raymond and I had known each other since we were little. Our moms were nurses at the same hospital, and when they used to hang out, we would too. Even after our moms' friendship had faded away, ours didn't.

"Yo, there's a party tonight. You tryna slide with me? It should be fun." Raymond seemed to be sitting on his couch and looked ready to go out.

"Damn a party? What time does it start?"

"At ten, bro, so you got an hour to get ready and get to my crib." As soon as he said it, I was conflicted. I was down to go out but knew I'd have to commit to a long-ass night.

Still, it didn't take a lot of convincing for me to give in. It wasn't like I was going to do anything better at home, "Alright, bet. I'll go. I'll see you there in a bit."

I hung up and went into the bathroom to fix my hair. Then, I went into my room down the hall and changed into a navy shirt. I kept my jeans on, though. I assumed the summer heat would diminish as it got later into the night. I grabbed my keys and was about to leave when Raymond Facetimed me again.

"Okay, so I forgot to mention that it's a pool party, so you better bring some swim shorts."

"Damn, after I just changed? Alright, I'll be at your crib in like twenty minutes. I'm about to leave."

"Bet, I'll see you then, Jayden," he said and then ended the call.

So, before I left, I went back into my room to change into my black swim shorts. I finally went down to my car, headed toward the lake, then sped away from Humboldt Park to Uptown. My family lived on the first floor of a three-story house that overlooked the park. Space was always tight because it was a small three-bedroom apartment. I shared it with my two younger sisters, Yomaira and Leyla, and our mom.

As I got closer to Raymond's house, I had the best view of the city's skyline. The light of the summer moon reflected onto the lake. Skyscrapers pressed next to each other in the heart of the city formed the bright skyline. This view was why I always liked visiting Raymond more than I liked him coming to me whenever we would hang out. Well, that was *one* of the reasons why I didn't want him coming over.

My neighborhood wasn't the safest. Humboldt Park is mostly known in Chicago for being a strong Puerto Rican community, but it's also home to a lot of Dominicans. Ever since my grandparents immigrated here, they made it their home.

Soon enough, I reached Raymond's apartment building that looked like it went up into to the sky. I parked in front of the building and texted Raymond to tell him I was outside. We decided to take his car, so if I drank, I could just crash at his place. He lived in the top floor of a thirty-story apartment building.

I walked through the big glass doors and through the lobby, which looked the same as when I first visited ten years before.

Mr. Lopez, the security guard at the front desk immediately greeted me. "Hello, Jayden, how are you tonight?"

"I'm good, Mr. Lopez. How are you?" He always had the warmest smile, and he'd been there forever, so he had everyone's names memorized.

"I'm doing well, son. You take care, alright?"

"You too," I replied.

Raymond walked out of the elevator and gestured for us to leave. "Bye, Mr. Lopez," he said as the door shut behind him.

We made our way to Raymond's car and hopped inside.

"So, how you been?" He started the car and headed north toward Lake Shore Drive.

"Been working all summer, man, that's why I've barely seen you these last few weeks. But what you been up to?" I reached for the aux and put on some music because I was not feeling what was on the radio.

"Working too. Tryna save up cause my six-month anniversary with Serenity is coming up and I don't know what to get her," he said, tapping his fingers on the steering wheel to the beat of the song.

"Damn, that's crazy. Six months? Shit, who would've known somebody would tie you down for this long."

"She's not just somebody, bro. I'm really not tryna fuck this up. It feels real with her."

I honestly thought he was doing too much, mostly because I was boycotting relationships and anything to do with love. "If she's the one, it doesn't sound like she's gonna let a present define y'all. Just get her something that has to do with the relationship."

"You right, it's just I was debating between a necklace and a ring," Raymond said as he reached for my phone to change the song.

He damn near gave me a heart attack right then and there. "A *ring*?"

"Damn, yeah. Why, is that doing too much?" He seemed nervous, like he was genuinely wondering. I wanted to scream, "Yes!" loud enough so that if I rolled the window down, the people leaving the beach could hear me.

Instead, I said, "I mean, boy, you better be thinking of an eighty-dollar Pandora ring, 'cause do I need to remind you, we are seventeen."

"Yeah, obviously not a nice-ass ring, but you think she'll like it?"

I wanted to nicely tell him to cool it and save the ring for the year mark, so I said, "No, yeah, she will, but I think a necklace would be better."

"Okay, what type of necklace?" He had his whole face scrunched up and went back to tapping his fingers on the wheel.

"You should get her your name or initial on it. I see that cute shit on Twitter all the time." I started getting hot, so I moved the air vent to hit my face directly.

"Damn, you lowkey right. I'mma drop some hints tonight and see what type of vibe she's giving me, necklace or ring."

"So, she gonna be there tonight? Finally I get to really meet her 'cause I only saw her once when I visited your school."

"Yeah, she's gonna be there with her best friend, Mariposa."

"Mariposa?" I had never met someone named after the Spanish word for butterfly. It was pretty.

"Yeah, why you say her name like that? You know her or something, Jayden?"

"Nah, I just never heard you mention her before. She cool?"

"No, yeah, she's chill as fuck. I got a feeling y'all gonna get along." Looking back now, he kinda called it before I even met her.

"Is it much farther?"

"No, we like two blocks away now, actually," Raymond said. It was hard not to notice that the houses had been getting bigger and nicer. A minute later, he drove up a driveway and parked next to a big garden. As soon as I stepped out of the car, I turned to Raymond wide-eyed and said, "Wow, this is insane."

He just looked at me and said, "I know. When I first came here, I couldn't believe it. Just wait, though. There's a pool out back and a full indoor basketball court."

It was the nicest house I had ever seen—a white mansion with a large marble staircase leading to a gold door. I could hear the music from outside, but none of the neighbors seemed to give a fuck; they were all on their balconies and porches drinking and eating. We started going up the staircase, but before we even got to the door, we heard two voices calling out, "Raymond!"

"Raymond! Wait up on us!" Serenity yelled.

"Hey, beautiful," Raymond said when he turned around and saw her. He instantly smiled. After they kissed hello, Serenity turned to me and said, "Hey, stranger, I haven't seen you in a minute. How you been?"

I shifted my weight back and forth. "I've been pretty good. Just been real busy with school and work." As I answered Serenity, Mariposa greeted Raymond. She then turned her focus to me. I said, "Hey, I'm Jayden. I haven't been able to meet you yet. You're Mariposa, right?"

She grinned with all her teeth, and I instantly felt like she had warmed the already hot summer night. "Yeah, I'm Mariposa, but you can call me Mari if you want. It's nice to meet you, Jayden. How do you know Raymond?"

"I'm damn near his cousin. Our moms worked together when we were younger, and we been friends ever since."

She laughed, and I found myself staring at her for a little too long. Besides her pretty smile, her entire face was the kind that you don't forget. She was kind of tall, but since I was six-foot three, I still had to look down to meet her big brown eyes. She had shiny, long dark brown hair that reached her waist. She was wearing a light blue sundress and Air Force 1s that were slightly beaten up.

Serenity was halfway through the door when she turned back to say, "We'll meet you guys inside, okay? Raymond just wants to say hi to a couple of friends." Before Mari could even answer, they were gone.

Mari grabbed my hand and took me up the stairs into the huge living room with chandeliers on the ceiling. "Come on, let's figure out where the drinks are at."

The room was dark with blue flashing lights blinking to the beat of the song. Probably forty people were already drunk and bumping into us in the living room as they jumped to the song. Mari said hi to a couple of people as we strolled to the back of the house and found a large red cooler filled with Modelos and Mike's Hards.

She grabbed a Modelo and handed me one. She shouted over the music, "Here, let's go out by the pool. I won't be able to hear you in here!" I followed her to the back porch where I could see at least fifty people hanging out both in and by the pool. We sat on a small blue bench that had a clear view of the backyard and living room.

Mari took a sip of her beer and made a face of disgust. She quickly turned to me with her big brown eyes and said, "So, what's on your mind?"

I can't lie—she for real caught me off guard. How was I supposed to answer a question like that? "Nothing really. I mean, why do you ask?"

She laughed softly and looked to the floor. "Yeah, I don't know. You seem like you got something on your mind. Why don't you first just tell me why you decided to pop out tonight?"

"Honestly, I had nothing else to do and it seemed like a better idea than just staying home alone." It was immediately easy to tell her the truth. I didn't feel the need to act like I didn't care what she thought.

"Oh, so you're an only child?"

I furrowed my eyebrows slightly, so she followed with, "Since, you say you would've been home alone. You don't got any siblings?"

Now her question made a lot more sense. I said, "No, I do. I got two younger sisters. They just weren't home. How about you?"

"Yeah, I got a twin brother, actually. He goes to our school, too. Should be around here somewhere. We just came at different times. This house is so damn big I ain't surprised I haven't seen him yet."

I looked around and saw bottles of expensive liquor and couldn't help but stare at the huge pool. "Nah, for real, can you imagine living in a house like this?"

"Hella kids from our school have it like this. It's crazy, but, hey—I ain't complaining. Right now, the view is pretty fucking great."

She took another sip of her beer, so I decided it was time to drink mine, too. As I drank, I looked at the Chicago skyline. I couldn't help but break into a grin and wonder, "So, is what we doing tonight asking each other real questions?"

She moved her knees to face me. "Yeah, what faster way to get to know someone than sharing our dreams and fears? It says a lot more than knowing someone's favorite color."

"Okay, so Mari, what's your wildest dream? Like if you could have anything in this world, what would you want?" She had me thinking about more than the party that surrounded us.

"I would want to fall in love and let it last me a lifetime," she said without hesitation and took another sip of beer. "What about you, what would you want out of life if it weren't so unfair?"

Her response surprised me, like how is it possible for someone to be so blunt and honest right off the bat? Her attitude was refreshing and contagious. "I don't think life is unfair. I think we often think we deserve more than we do, so we're disappointed with the shit that's thrown at us. It's all for a reason. Every struggle forces us to grow up and learn. Honestly, I think the people who have it the most fucked up are the luckiest because they end up the strongest. When they get through the final test, they gonna live their best life. But, about love, you ain't missing out, girl; that shit's for fools."

I think what I immediately liked most about her was how she didn't get mad when we disagreed. She didn't even make it seem like she thought she was right. She was just genuinely curious. She took another small sip of her beer and said, "Why do you say that?"

"I fell in love with this girl, gave her a year of my life, and she broke my heart. She cheated on me, and ever since then, that shit's dead to me." After I said that, all I could think was, "*Fuck, did I really say that?*"

She turned to me with the saddest eyes and said, "Damn, Jayden, I'm sorry. That sucks, but I don't know. I've only had shitty-ass experiences with guys so far. I don't think I've ever really been in love, but I guess I'm holding out some hope. I just want something out of a movie to happen to me, you know? But at the same time, I stop everything before it even gets close to something real, so I don't know how I expect to have my fairy tale like that." She laughed softly to herself at the end.

She looked so damn beautiful, but my dumb ass still went and said, "I ain't looking for love. That's all I can really say."

She took another sip and then motioned to Serenity and Raymond with her bottle. They were talking and swimming in the pool. "What about them? Do you believe in them?"

"I know that boy is in love by the way he talks to me about Serenity. But we ain't them, so who are we to even say whether their feelings are real or not? They're obviously together for a reason." I meant it, too. The conversation I had with Raymond in the car just further proved his feelings.

"Yeah, just look at the way they stare at each other as if they could be happy for the rest of their lives, even if that was all they did." A sigh escaped her lips as she looked at them.

I couldn't help but think that I wouldn't mind staring at her forever, but I said nothing and chugged the beer. I got up to go throw the can into the trash bag and was about to ask Mari something else when police sirens started blaring.

Everyone started screaming, "Twelve! Run!" Soon, loud, drunk teenagers completely surrounded me. I felt Mari pull my hand and lead me through the crowd. "Come on. We gotta run. When everything cools down, we'll meet up with Serenity and Raymond."

She didn't seem scared, just determined. It helped that I had been to a lot of parties that had gotten popped before, even if that one was different. I really knew no one except for Raymond, and we were in a fancy white neighborhood. The cops would definitely run after the tall brown man.

We ran for a couple of minutes through streets filled with mansions just as big or even bigger than the one we came from. We finally stopped to figure out where to wait for Raymond and Serenity to come pick us up. We sat on the edge of the sidewalk facing a small playground. Out of breath, Mari looked at me and started laughing. "Damn, these white people sure know how to throw a memorable party, huh? Sorry I had to pull you like that, but I didn't wanna lose you in the crowd. Did I hurt you?" She grabbed my hand and held it for a second.

I couldn't help but laugh with her even though the cops had me a bit shaken up. "Nah, don't worry. You ain't hurt me." I was about to tell her how beautiful she looked when rain started to fall. Honestly, it felt good as fuck because the run had us both sweating.

She looked up at the sky, closed her eyes, and smiled. "You know, I love rain."

"Really? I've never been a fan; it reminds me of sadness," I said, but I followed her lead and let the rain fall on my face.

"No, it doesn't have to be sad. It's romantic. It's like all of those damn movies where the two main characters fall in love and kiss in the rain."

As soon as she said that, all I wanted to do was pull her close to me and be the one she kissed in the rain. But instead, I said, "I don't think it really has anything to do with the rain."

She playfully moved closer to my face. "Obviously not, but it makes the moment feel raw, real, and almost desperate. Like they needed to kiss so bad that they said fuck the rain."

I didn't know how to tell her I didn't think the rain had anything to do with me wanting to kiss her, so I chose to not say anything. She was being really honest. She said she was looking for love, and I wasn't.

I was stuck on what to say or do, but I lost my chance because Raymond was pulling up in his car. We had to run across the street to get in, and before I opened the door for her, she said, "I'm glad you decided to come."

We went through the McDonalds drive thru, making conversation about anything and everything. After we dropped Serenity and Mari off, it was just me and Raymond in the car. We rode in silence, each of us thinking about a certain girl.

He dropped me off at my car in his parking lot and that was it—the end to a great night that left me with Mariposa stuck in my head.

* * *

JUNE 2019

Serenity snapped me back into reality because she was losing her shit in the kitchen, yelling about the speaker not being loud enough. At this point, I think even Elijah could tell it didn't have shit to do with the speaker.

"Yo, Serenity! Girl, don't worry if the speaker ain't loud enough. Raymond can go pick mine up at my crib. But lowkey, this one's more than loud enough. What, you want your neighbors to hear it too?" I said, trying to break the tension.

She took some deep breaths and tried to relax. "Yeah, I know. You right. Everything is going to be okay. I think we're all ready now, so this gives us girls like an hour or so to get ready." She looked at Mari and then the clock.

Mari took Serenity to the hallway toward the bedroom. She patted Serenity's back and said, "Yeah, come on now. Go take a shower. You'll feel better, I promise. Once you come out, I'll take a quick shower too and get ready with you."

Serenity listened to her and went to her room. Mari came and sat next to me on the couch. "I'mma have to beat Raymond's ass when he gets here, 'cause why's he getting her all worried and stressed out on her birthday?"

"What he do?" asked Elijah, who was barely paying attention. He'd been texting and staring at his phone ever since I picked him up. I'd lowkey been meaning to ask him if he got a new girl or sum.

"No, nothing serious. He just acting a little shady. Probably tryna surprise her with his gift, but you know how she is about surprises."

Mari laughed softly and then turned to me and playfully punched my arm. "You gotta get your man to get his ass over here, boy."

I could tell she didn't believe what she was saying about Raymond and that she genuinely wanted him to get here fast. I was just glad that we were still good enough to joke around with each other. "Don't worry, princess! Your prince is on it."

She gave me a small smile. Elijah still barely looked up to say, "There we go again, Jayden. She don't want your ass."

We all laughed. "Yeah, I know."

Mari turned to face me when I said that and just looked at me with those big brown eyes of hers. It only hurts because of how good it used to be, like on our first date. It may sound cheesy, but I'd be lying if I didn't admit it was magical.

* * *

JUNE 2018

I had finally kissed her last night after having wanted to since almost a year ago when I met her. I honestly could barely sleep. I was running through the night in my mind over and over, trying to figure out what it all meant.

I hadn't given her many details about what we were doing tonight. I just told her to get ready for a night of adventure and that I would pick her up at 6:00 p.m. I got to her crib five minutes early and texted her if she was ready. She replied, "*Yeah, be out in a minute.*"

When she walked out, I was in shock. Even though I had picked her up countless times before, I hadn't ever let myself see her in any way other than my close friend. She somehow looked more even beautiful tonight than she had the night before. I got out of the car to open the door for her.

I said, "Wow, you look amazing." She had on a light pink floral sundress with white sandals and a small white purse. Her hair was down in loose curls, and she had two white hair clips on the sides.

She hugged me. "Thank you. You clean up well, too. I see you!" She smelled like cocoa butter.

Once we got in the car and pulled out of her driveway, she asked, "So, what we doing today, Jayden?"

I couldn't help but laugh. "Well, actually, if you don't mind, it's a surprise." I adjusted her air vent so it wouldn't hit her directly in the face.

"Can it really be a surprise, though? We've gone out to eat so many times, Jayden, I feel like we're running out of places." She naturally took control over my aux and let her music cut the nervousness in the car.

I wondered if she was as confused as I was. I knew I wanted to be with her but didn't know if I could be in a relationship with labels, expectations, and—most of the time—disappointments. I said, "Yeah, 'cause today's different."

"Alright, I'm down then. Try your best to surprise me."

We drove for a while bumping reggaetón. I had a million things on my mind, and they brought me back to the question of what I was going to do. "We're here," I announced as I got to the parking lot of a burger joint. "Small Cheval."

Her eyes widened and she smiled at me with her whole face. "Ooh, damn. You did surprise me! Didn't I mention this place to you like a month ago?"

"Yeah, I remembered. But don't forget—this is only the first stop on our adventure." I got out of the car to meet her on the passenger side and help her out. Before that, I opened the trunk to get one of the three roses I had bought. I opened the door and held it up so she could grab it from my hand.

"Wow, it's beautiful and baby pink. How'd you know that's the color I'd wear tonight?"

"What can I say, that's just how well I know you." Little did she know I bought the cheapest ones I could find. I had just finished covering rent, electricity, and water for the month, meaning I barely had enough for this date.

"You're sweet, Jayden. So unlike you," she teased.

After we ordered, I grabbed our food and we walked to one of the tables outside. While we ate, we watched the sun start to set.

"So, you told Elijah anything yet? Just give me the heads up on whether he's trying to beat my ass or not."

She laughed. "Nah, I mean, I guess there's not much to say yet, right?" Her entire energy was contagious, as was her honesty.

"Yeah, true. I know we know each other already, but like with a real first date, I think we gotta start with the basics." I took a bite of my burger.

She raised her eyebrow and gave me a sly look. "Okay, and what would those be?" She looked down at her food and finished the last bite.

I said, "I'mma start you off easy. What's your favorite color?"

"Easy. It's dark royal blue, the color of the sky right before it turns black. How about you?"

"Red, nothing in particular about it. I just like the way it looks. Now, it's your turn to ask me a question, but let's get in the car and go to the second stop of our adventure before it gets too late." I picked up our trash and went to throw it out.

We walked back to my car and once we were back on the road, she said, "Okay, you got any random talents?"

"Umm, damn, I don't know. I guess I learned how to play piano when I was younger, but I also really like soccer. I don't know if I'm necessarily talented, but. . . You?"

"I used to paint and draw. Not so much anymore, though." We were stuck at a red light and I couldn't help staring at her.

Before answering, she caught me looking. "Why you looking at me like that?" She laughed softly and immediately turned red.

"I guess I can't help looking at you. You're so beautiful." I wanted to kiss her right then and there.

She laughed again, still flushed. She said, "You're a fool, Jayden." A car behind us started honking, and we both looked to see the light had turned green. "See, you gonna get us killed."

Laughing along with her, I pulled into a parking spot next to La Michoacana on Lawrence and Kedzie. "Looking at you would make it worth it though. We're here now." This had always been my favorite ice cream shop on the northside. Raymond's parents used to bring us here all the time.

Her eyes lit up. "Jayden, stop playing. You already know La Michoacana is the way to my heart."

I got out of the car and went to the trunk to get the second pink rose. I opened her door, and before I could say anything, she said, "It's beautiful, thank you."

"I was gonna save it for my date later tonight, but I decided I had to give you two 'cause I'm in the presence of an artist," I said, laughing.

She immediately laughed. "Boy, shut up! You playing with me, talking about having another date tonight." She understood my sense of humor. It was one of many reasons why I fell for her so hard the past year.

"See, I didn't know you were into art. I would love to see your work soon. I'm sure you're better than you think." I held her hand and led her from my car to the counter inside the shop.

Once it was our turn in line, we both picked *mangonadas* and waited against the wall for them to call our order.

"Now, we gonna take this and eat it at the third location of our adventure. But back to the questions. Now answer this: where would you want to travel to if you could go anywhere?"

"You know you really good at planning dates. You get your inspiration from your past or from the movies like me?" She laughed quietly before saying, "Anyway, I'd go to Amsterdam. You?"

"Thanks, but no, yeah, I loved planning dates for my ex. Romantic comedies can be pretty good too. I'll deny it if you tell anyone though. I'd go to Bali. It just looks beautiful," I replied as they called our order.

Once we got on the road again, she looked out the window at the pedestrians walking by. "Tell me, Jayden. I don't think I've ever asked who your favorite artist is."

"Easy, Brent Faiyaz. He knows how to make you feel something with his words. I know yours is Frank Ocean, so I'm not even going to start." I laughed, teasing her.

She gasped, pretending to take offense. "I only defend him so hard because he's truly a lyrical genius, in my humblest opinion. I would give so much money to see him live, you don't understand. Money I definitely don't have, either."

I rolled my eyes. "Yeah, yeah, I know."

She smiled. "I tell Serenity all the time, you know, that the best music is the saddest 'cause that's what feels the realest. Wait. . . are you taking me where I think you are?"

"Guess," I said.

"Montrose Beach?" she asked with the biggest smile on her face.

"Yep!" I said as I parked the car and went to get the final rose from the trunk. I opened the door for her, and she looked just as happy as she did when she saw the first rose.

"Thank you, Jayden. You already know this is my favorite place in the whole city."

"I mean, I knew you liked it, but why's it your favorite?"

"It's just so damn pretty the way the lake and the skyline meet. There's also the harbor where you can just be alone with your thoughts and the beauty of the city. Plus, it's far enough from the city lights that you can still see some stars."

"Yeah, I know. It's so peaceful. I come here alone whenever I need to think things through. I've never taken anyone here on a date. I was saving it for someone special—someone like you, Mari."

I got a blanket from my car, and we lay next to each other while we played our favorite albums by our favorite artists. It was just us listening to music and searching for specks in the sky, wondering whether they were planes or stars. She played songs from Blond, and I played others from Sonder Son.

I knew we'd have to leave soon because I didn't want to get her home too late. It was nearing 10:30 p.m. when I turned to face her big, pretty brown eyes. "I'm really glad I finally kissed you last night."

She smiled and turned. Our noses were an inch away from each other. She just said, "Me too."

I grabbed her face softly and kissed her again, but this time was different from the night before. This time, it was more desperate, more passionate, less innocent, and more urgent. We kissed for a couple minutes, and then she said, "You know, my parents are gonna start worrying soon, even if they know I'm with you."

"Yeah, come on now. Let me take you home." I held her hand as I grabbed the blanket, and we went back to the car.

We spent five hours together that night, but it only felt like one. Time always flew when I was with her.

* * *

JUNE 2019

She was always honest and direct. Her words reminded me of how different it was between us now. She woke me from my daydream when she asked, "Jayden, why've you been staring?"

"Guess I can't help it, butterfly," I said, fully knowing why. I just looked at the floor because I couldn't keep looking her in the eyes.

After all, it's my fault. It's so complicated between us now. I should've been more honest like her, and maybe we wouldn't have to still be a secret a year later.

IV.

ELIJAH

"Happy Break up Song" - Femdot

when we are young
we feel invincible even when everything and everyone
around is reminding us
we are far from it
but it feels easier to lie to ourselves than to face that ugly
truth
that we are not invincible
and frankly bad liars, too.

- ESTHER HUESCAS

JUNE 2019

"I honestly don't get y'all," I said as I looked at Jayden, who was making it painfully obvious that he was still in love with Mari. Mari, too, was easy as fuck to read, although I may have just thought that because she's my twin. They'd never admit it, but I know something happened between them last summer. Sometimes I think about confronting Mari about it, but she deserves to have a secret too, God knows I haven't told her about mine.

"There's nothing to get, Elijah. Jayden just likes to play too much," Mari snapped.

Damn, that one had to hurt. They continued with their painfully obvious comments, and I went back to my phone. Honestly, I'd been distracted all day because I knew the person I'd been texting was coming to the party that night. That's why I was really happy when I heard the soccer game got canceled. Of course, I wanted to help Serenity with the prep work, but secretly, I also needed to make sure I figured out how to hang out with them without anyone seeing us—especially my sister.

"So, Elijah what you tryna do in the meantime while the girls get ready?" Jayden asked.

"I'm down for anything, man." I just wanted to find any excuse to stop thinking about the night ahead of me.

"You tryna smoke?" Jayden asked.

"Yeah, I'm down to in a bit."

"Okay, bet," Jayden said.

* * *

JULY 2017

The first time I smoked weed was the summer between my sophomore and junior years when our friend group had started hanging out more.

We lived in a small, two-story house in Belmont Cragin on the northwest side of Chicago. Our parents were rarely home during the day because they worked all the time. So, that summer, when we and our friends weren't working, everyone would come over to our place.

It was a Saturday around noon when I opened the door. "Hey, you must be Jayden. I'm Elijah, Mari's brother," I said and led him to the living room where we were all already hanging out.

"What's up, man? Nice to meet you. Thanks for the invite, too. I appreciate it," he said in a deep voice.

"No problem. If you want a beer, they in the fridge. Then you can meet up with us in the living room. It's just down the hall."

"Okay, yeah, sounds good," Jayden said as he watched Mari bounce down the stairs from her room, almost on cue to his arrival.

She smiled as soon as she saw him and greeted him with a hug. I left through the hall to go the living room.

They ended up coming to meet us in the living room a couple minutes later. Serenity and Raymond had been dating for a couple of months, but they never made it awkward when anyone else was in the room. It was like they were just best friends who happened to be dating.

"Jayden, welcome to the infamous kickbacks at the Marquez crib," said Raymond, waving his arms triumphantly in the air.

"Thanks, man. Your house is nice as fuck, guys," Jayden said to Mari and me.

"Thanks. The backyard is the best though, you'll love it," Mari answered.

"As a thank you for inviting me to one of your infamous kickbacks, I brought a little gift for all of us to share," Jayden said, holding up a bag with three joints in them.

"Merch, you brought some weed!" Raymond said excitedly, hopping off the couch.

"Yeah, y'all smoke?" Jayden asked me, Serenity, and Mari.

"I do! Not often, but I'm down. Elijah doesn't smoke, though, so count him out," Mari said. She and our cousins smoked whenever they came over, but I never saw the appeal in trying it.

"I don't," Serenity said.

I rolled my eyes at Mari and blurted out, "Never done it before, but you know what, Mari? I'mma try it today. Why not?"

"Okay, let's go out. Now I can see your backyard." Jayden winked at Mari.

We all went to our backyard where we had a swing chair and two outdoor couches surrounding a fireplace. Mari sat on the swing, Jayden and I sat on one couch, and Serenity and Raymond sat on the other one.

Jayden pulled the first joint out of the bag and lit it up while Mari put on some music.

Jayden took the first hit as I said, "So, y'all want to watch a movie after this?"

"Oh, yes, and we're gonna have to go to the corner store to get some snacks too." Mari took the joint from Jayden and hit it next.

"I'll talk to the cashier when we go 'cause I can't have y'all making a fool out of yourselves," said Serenity, laughing.

We all laughed at the thought of us speaking gibberish to the poor cashier. I said, "No one cares over here, though. I swear these corner stores damn near expect people to come in fucked up. Every time I walk in there, everyone but me seems to be high or drunk. Y'all know that's how the hood is." I took the joint from Mari's hand. "So, I just suck and hold it, or what?"

"Yeah and then after, you breathe the smoke in as much as you can, then let it out," said Jayden.

I did as he said and let the smoke out through my nose. I immediately started to cough. Mid-attack, I passed the joint to Raymond.

"It's okay. When it goes down the wrong way, you start coughing hard as fuck," said Mari. We passed around two of the joints until my entire body felt like it was vibrating. We decided to save the third one for the next kickback and go to the corner store to get some food.

"Okay, ladies and gentlemen, follow me. I'm about to help your high asses out and get y'all to the nearest bags of chips," said Serenity as she led us out the door and toward the end of the block. It was the slowest forty-second walk I had ever experienced.

When we got to the store, I grabbed a bag of Takis Fuego, a bag of Cheeto Puffs, and a large Sprite we all decided we were going to share. I turned around and saw everyone else getting so many bags of chips. The guy at the counter looked at us and started laughing. As Serenity promised, she was the one who did the talking.

"That'll be $22.14," the cashier said.

"Okay, here you go," Serenity said as she handed him her card.

The cashier handed her card back and said, "Y'all be safe out there."

We all thanked him in unison and heard him laughing as we walked out. Serenity led us back to the house and set us up on the couch to watch a movie. She gave everyone their bags of chips and brought cups for the Sprite from the kitchen. We spent the rest of the afternoon until the sun started to set just watching movies on Netflix. The high wore off just as our parents came home.

"Hi, kids!" said my mom as she walked in and saw us all watching movies.

"Hi, Mrs. Marquez," said all our friends in unison as Mari and I went up to greet her and my dad, who was getting the last of the groceries from the car.

When my dad walked in, he asked, "Hi, guys! Have you been watching movies all day?"

"Yes. Hi, Mr. Marquez," they said again, almost in unison.

My mom suggested we make s'mores by the fireplace, and Serenity decided to spend the night since it was getting late. Meanwhile, Raymond and Jayden lived closer so they said they would just leave afterward.

That was the first day we had all spent together. After two years, I think we've probably spent close to 100 days at our house. I think what works about us is that while we're all close, we each have our secrets that we know how to put aside when we all come together.

* * *

JUNE 2019

"Okay, guys, Serenity just texted me saying she's done showering, so I'mma go hop in and get ready. I'll see you guys in an hour, looking like a new woman." Mari winked as she hopped off the couch and skipped down the hallway to Serenity's room.

"Come on, Elijah, let's go, too. By the time we come back, the girls will be done." Jayden got up and headed down the hallway to the back door.

"You right, we gotta pass the time," I said, following him.

Serenity's backyard had a couple of comfy seats and a hammock. We both opted for the seats.

Jayden pulled out a blunt and lit it up. "So, I was about to say something in front of Mari in there, but I don't know what the vibe is. Sorry, I'm just curious—I gotta know. You talking to a new girl or what, man? You been glued to your phone since I picked you up."

"Yeah, something like that." I took the blunt from him and hit it. I'd been trying not to smoke so much these days because of soccer. If I decide to keep playing in college on the club team, they do drug tests.

"Damn, so you into her or what? Bro, if anything, you should invite her tonight. You can get to her and shit! You never know, maybe it can lead to something else. Shit, even for a little stress reliever. You've been telling me the team has been driving you crazy." Jayden reached for the blunt.

"Yeah, the team has been driving me crazy because the guy I like is on it. All I want to do is jump on top of him in practice and kiss him. That's what's annoying, not the team."

I laughed. "Man, why you so interested in who I'm texting? How about you finally be honest with me about how you feel about my sister?"

Jayden's eyes widened, and he looked at the ground. "What? Nothing's going on." He shifted uncomfortably in his seat.

"Yeah, that's what I thought. You keep your secret, and I'll keep mine."

"Yeah, okay, whatever. Pretend I never asked, okay?" Jayden shrugged.

I didn't mean to snap on Jayden. He'd honestly become my best friend, besides Mariposa. There had been so many times within the last year that I genuinely thought I was going to tell him I'm gay, but something always got in the way. Honestly, I always got in my own way.

I thought I was really ready to tell him after I had my first date with a guy a year ago.

***

JULY 2018

Last summer, I downloaded Tinder. Honestly, I did it mostly for entertainment purposes, but also because I'd started to become more comfortable with being gay. So, I made a profile and pretended like I was eighteen when really, I was seventeen. I knew that was wrong, but I felt like it was my only choice. I needed confirmation that what I was feeling was normal.

I started swiping and then after a little while, I got a match. He was cute, had just turned eighteen, and had been held back a year, which meant he was going to start his senior year of high school in the fall. I knew that it was unlikely I would ever have to see him again because he lived in the suburbs. We started talking and agreed to meet up for coffee in Wicker Park.

I told my parents and Mari that I was meeting with a friend from school for lunch, and they didn't really ask any questions. Mari did notice the effort I was putting into getting ready, so she assumed I was going on a date. When she asked me, I just lied because I was embarrassed. I'm sure she assumed I was going a date with a girl.

When I got to the coffee shop, I immediately saw the guy from Tinder. He was tall and handsome and had a warm smile. He got up from the booth and hugged me hello.

"Hey, I'm Andres. It's nice to finally meet you, Elijah." His voice was raspy but soothing.

"Hey, Andres, I'm glad we finally met up, too." I was still analyzing his features as I responded. His cheekbones seemed as if they were carved out, and his lips were full and shiny.

"Do you want to get something before you sit down?" Andres asked.

"Yeah, I'll be right back. I'm just going to get a coffee and a cookie." I set my book bag onto the floor by my chair.

"Okay, I'll be here," he said as he pulled out a book and started to read. He looked so cool and collected. Meanwhile, I was sweating bullets, not just because of the sunlight pouring through the window.

I walked up to the counter and ordered a small black coffee and an oatmeal cookie. While I waited, I couldn't help but notice how cool the entire cafe was. The design was around old school comic books, and all the drinks and furniture fit the theme.

They called my order, I grabbed it, and sat across from Andres. "So, have you come to this cafe before? I love the theme." With my coffee and cookie in my hands, I felt more comfortable with the entire situation.

"Yeah, I come here whenever I decide to come down to the city. I only live like thirty minutes from the city limits, but I rarely come down unless there's a reason to."

"So, you prefer the suburbs?" I asked.

"Yeah, I've never really known anything different, but I do love it. It's quiet and everything that's not in town is close enough with a car. But how about you? Do you like living in the city?"

"Oh, yeah, I love it. I wouldn't know how to deal with the suburbs 'cause I'm so used to the noise and how many people there always are around you."

"I mean one thing's for sure: it's a lot easier to be openly gay in a city versus in a suburb. At least in a city, there's so many damn people most of the time you can hide in the numbers. There are places that feel safe, like this café. It's my little safe haven in Chicago. Do you have a favorite first date spot?" he asked and stared into my eyes.

My palms were sweating. "I don't know. I don't really go on dates like that."

"Oh, why? You too much of a player?" Andres teased.

I wasn't planning on being so honest, but I felt like I should return the favor since he seemed genuine. "Well, no, it's because this is my first date with a guy. But this is really nice." I smiled at Andres and met his eyes, which were a mesmerizing shade of green.

"Oh, cool, so you're bisexual?" He leaned toward me. I didn't get the vibe that he was judging me, just that he was curious.

I smiled softly. "No, I'm gay. I just haven't come out to anyone yet, so I tried dating girls for a while. It just didn't go so well." I looked down at my hands.

"When I went on my first date, I was a nervous wreck. He was nice and all, but we just had nothing to talk about besides the book I was reading. It would've been fine if I hadn't just barely started it. He ended up spoiling the whole series for me. Not the best date, but it definitely left me with a fun story to tell." Andres let out a soft snort.

"I guess that's a pretty nice way at looking at it. I should be more positive like that. Any other advice for me?" I asked half-jokingly, but I was glad I did.

He took a big sip of his drink and then answered, "I mean, I know how hard it is to not be able to openly be yourself. I barely came out to everyone in my family a year ago. It was hard, but I'm thankful they're loving. I hope whenever you do decide to come out, it turns out like that for you. Trust me, I know it seems like the scariest thing in the world, but once you doit, it's so liberating."

"Yeah, part of me feels guilty for not telling my best friends. I feel like I damn near owe it to them because of how close we are, but I know you're right. I'll tell them when I'm ready." At that moment, I wasn't holding anything back. I wanted to live a couple of hours in full honesty.

"So, this is your first date, you say?" Andres reached over the booth to hold my hand. "Am I doing an okay job?"

I laughed. "Yes. Seriously, thank you for all the advice and for letting me be honest about everything."

He let go of my hand to take a sip from his latte and looked up to meet my eyes when he was done. With a warm smile, he said, "I'm gonna show you the best first date so you won't have an awkward story to tell your friends when you come out."

I laughed and finished my coffee. "Okay. Bring it on, Andres."

We got up, picked up our trash, and threw it out before exiting to the busy street filled with hipsters in their twenties. He grabbed my hand, which felt nice but also immensely terrifying; I was showcasing how I felt for the first time in public. I felt braver because of how normal Andres made it seem, so I followed his lead.

We went into a small, old bookstore. The walls were completely covered in old movie and music posters, the ceilings were high, and big old chairs were scattered throughout the store. People stood lost in the aisles reading the book jackets of anything that caught their eyes. No one even seemed to care that two guys were holding hands. Andres took me to the back of the store to the fantasy novels and put three books in my hand.

Andres tapped the top book. "These right here will get you hooked on reading, I swear. Plus, they're all used so these three books cost less than ten dollars. Isn't that crazy?"

"Yeah, it's crazy. Thank you so much for this."

"I told you, I'm going to give you a date worthy of telling, Elijah—"

Before he could finish, I leaned in and kissed him softly and quickly. I couldn't help remember that I had to go back to reality in a couple hours. Even if I fell in love with Andres, I couldn't take him home to meet my parents or my friends without lying about who he was. I realized that I couldn't see him often even if I wanted to because he lived far away. I also remembered I had lied about my age. On all the Tinder dates I'd go on—no matter how perfect—I could never really be fully honest. Not right now. So, I pulled back.

"Why'd you stop? Today, while you're with me, we can pretend that nothing else matters except this date. Okay, Elijah?"

"Okay, Andres." I was about to turn around to go pay for the books when he grabbed my cheek and led my lips to his. This time, I didn't pull back. I let the fantasy come true. His shiny lips were just as soft as they looked. His chest pressed against me firmly but tenderly at the same time. He smelled of men's cologne, and it overpowered me in the best way. I didn't want the moment to ever end.

* * *

JUNE 2019

I never saw Andres again after that day. We texted for a few months afterward, but once the summer ended, we both got busier.

I knew Mari wouldn't care that I was gay, but it would break her heart that I hadn't told her before. I knew she'd feel bad because she'd think it was her fault that I couldn't trust her, when it really had nothing to do with me not trusting her and everything to do with my irrational fear of being rejected. I also had a rational fear of being hurt, because being a gay Mexican man in America didn't really get you that many fans.

Before I knew it, I was high as fuck. The only thing I could think about was how the hell I was going to be able to have fun with my crush, Diego, without anyone else noticing tonight.

"Lowkey, Elijah, I don't even know who's coming to this party. I feel like random people from school will wanna show up." Jayden scratched his chin.

"Yeah, I invited Diego, my friend from my soccer team. I feel like he'll have a good time." I shivered when I said my crush's name.

"Diego? I've never heard you mention him. He cool?" Jayden had no idea that I hadn't mentioned him because I wanted to hook up with him, not bring him to drink a beer with us.

"Yeah, he's chill. You'll meet him tonight. I'll probably be with him the whole night," I murmured. I decided the best way to avoid potentially making it suspicious was to divert the attention away from me, so I said, "How about you, Jayden, you gonna be looking for anyone tonight? You know, besides my sister?"

He laughed nervously. "Nah, man. I'm not really trying to find anyone right now. These girls. . . they're all the same." I didn't expect him to completely ignore the comment about Mari again, but I took it as a sign that he was really going through it.

"Let's go back to the living room. I think the girls are gonna be ready soon. I also gotta figure out where the hell Raymond is 'cause it's past nine now." Jayden shook his head.

"Yeah, you right. Come on." I led the way through the back door and into the living room where Mari was hanging up a *Happy Birthday* sign.

"Wow, Mari, you look stunning," said Jayden after his jaw physically dropped. My sister had on a bodycon red dress and had made her long, black hair wavy. She wore her trusty white Vans that made her look effortlessly pretty.

"Seriously, Mari, wow. I think you're definitely the better-looking twin tonight."

She laughed. "Oh, my god, you guys are too much. And Elijah, why you lying to yourself? I'm always the hotter twin." She laughed and hugged me. "But, also, guys, Serenity looks so good! Y'all ain't gonna believe it 'til you see it. Serenity, come out!"

Jayden and I sat down next to each on the couch before Serenity came out.

She stepped out of her room wearing a sleek black dress that made her look beautiful and classy, but her accessories made her the clear birthday girl. She had on sparkly silver heels, a sparkly necklace, and dangling diamond earrings. Her braids came down to her waist, and she wore dark red lipstick that would make sure everyone knew she was the birthday girl if everything else wasn't telling them yet.

"Serenity, you look amazing! Raymond is going to lose his mind when he sees you," Jayden commented.

Mari and I simultaneously glared at Jayden for mentioning Raymond hadn't shown up yet. Serenity immediately looked down at her phone to see if Raymond had responded to her dozens of texts.

In an effort to distract her, I pointed out the obvious. "Serenity, you look beautiful."

"Damn, no, yeah, you guys are the sweetest. I love you all! But I'm about to lose my mind over Raymond, not the other way around," Serenity said. She and Mari walked back to Serenity's room so they could both keep trying his phone.

I looked down at my phone and saw a message from Diego that read, "*I can't wait to see u! Let's do what we been wanting to do all season, tonight ;)*"

I replied with, "*Can't wait! ;)*"

I didn't know what to do, though. I worried about how I was going to be able to do what I wanted without anyone noticing. I needed more than the original forty people that Serenity invited to show up in order to get away with anything. I was busy overthinking when I noticed Jayden's phone buzzed. When he glanced down at his phone, he looked very concerned.

I whispered, "Everything okay?"

He just showed me his phone, and it was text from Raymond.

The message read. "*I ran into Edwin after I got Serenity's present. We got to talking about the party, and he said he's coming and bringing some others. Serenity's going to kill me when she finds out Edwin's coming along. Bro, what she gonna say if his crew shows up? What if he brings Valeria too? Fuck do I do, Jayden?*"

All I could manage to whisper back to Jayden was, "Damn it, Raymond."

"I know, but we can't tell Mari or Serenity. Not yet. Let him be the one to explain. I'm just gonna tell him to get here as fast as possible," whispered Jayden.

V.

RAYMOND

"BROKEN GIRLS" - Saba

I'm not in the business of losing my mind over some pretty eyes as they look at me
yet something about your eyes mesmerize me
they look right through me
I like the way you look at me like I'm made of glass
I hate the way you treat me
like glass doesn't break
knowing damn well it does
I hate the way you're okay with breaking me,
pretty eyes.

- ESTHER HUESCAS

APRIL 2019

Mari and I were in the kitchen alone during one of our group hangouts at her house. She was washing some strawberries for us to eat when I asked her, "Mari, you mind helping me figure out what to get Serenity for her birthday?"

Her eyes immediately lit up, and she stopped washing the fruit to help. "Of course! You got any ideas or no?"

"Yeah, I mean, I was thinking about some sort of jewelry for the main gift and then I'll give her eighteen peonies to continue our cheesy tradition." I couldn't help but smile as I thought back to the tradition I started on her sixteenth birthday of getting her the same number of peonies as her age. Peonies had been her favorite flower ever since she was little because her mom grew them in their backyard every season.

"I love y'all's relationship for real. I definitely think you shouldn't get her a necklace 'cause, you know, she already has one of her name that you got her a while back. What about a bracelet?"

I whispered to make sure Serenity wouldn't hear from the living room, "I was actually thinking about a ring. Do you think she would think it's too much?"

Her face scrunched up. "It's only too much if you make it something really big. But I mean, you gotta figure out what you want it to mean."

"I don't really know yet, just tryna show her I love her for real," I lied. I knew what I wanted it to mean. I wanted to give her a promise ring before she went to Columbia in the fall. I hoped that I would hear back from NYU soon, but I knew I had to figure out my shit before I told her best friend my plans.

I could feel her staring at me hard, probably wondering what I was holding back. Mari said, "Well, that's sweet, but no matter what, you gotta remember Serenity already knows that."

"I appreciate that, Mari. Do you know what stone she'd like best?"

She pressed her lips together. "I mean, I don't think she has a favorite one. Diamonds are beautiful, but what about her birthstone? I don't know it off the top of my head, but I feel like it would be more personal."

"Damn, Mari, what's taking you so long? You growing the berries, too?" yelled Elijah from the living room.

Mari laughed. "Shut up, Elijah. You tryna come wash them yourself?"

"Yeah, let's go back. Thank you, though. I'mma search up the stone and figure out where to get it."

"Yeah, no problem. True, we definitely gotta get back before Serenity starts asking questions," Mari said.

I always knew that she had Serenity's best interests at heart. I was grateful to have such a solid group of people by my side. I couldn't imagine how different everything would be in the fall.

* * *

JUNE 2019

I was driving and listening to some music as I tried not to overthink about Serenity's present on the drive from Bronzeville to Little Village. It turned out that her birthstone was alexandrite, and I was driving to the only shop that carried an alexandrite ring for less than a thousand dollars. Just a week before, I was ready to give up on the stone and go for something cheaper, but I got lucky at the shop. The ring had a thin gold band, the bright purple-blue gem, and a small diamond on either side. I bought it immediately once the salesman told me it would cost three hundred for the ring and fifty more for a band adjustment. I agreed to pick it up in a week on her birthday.

I was nervous but hyped for the night. I couldn't wait to see Serenity relaxed after stressing so much these last few months over college applications. We lowkey hadn't been in the best place with our relationship, but I thought she was just scared about what going to New York City would mean for us. Since both of us had been applying to schools, we couldn't spend much time with each other. I could sense we were both trying to figure out what the other person wanted after the summer. I wondered if me wanting to be with her was enough.

I had barely gotten to the shop when my phone buzzed and I saw a message from Jayden. "*Yo, come out, man, I just got to Serenity's crib.*"

Damn, I'd been thinking so much about Serenity's gift, I forgot I told Jayden I'd help unload the drinks. I replied, "*Man, my bad. I'm picking up her gift. I'll be there in an hour. Just text Mari to come help y'all with the drinks.*"

Jayden said, "*Yeah I'mma just call out to them so they can both come help. I'm with Elijah, too.*"

I didn't know why Jayden didn't want to just text or call Mari instead of yelling to them. Jayden could act so weird when it came to Mari, but honestly, I'd never really thought about it much. I made a mental note to ask him about it at the party that night. "*Bet. I'll see y'all in a bit.*"

As I got deeper into Little Village, Mexican flags and images of the Virgin of Guadalupe surrounded me and the smell of sweet bread and fresh tortillas filled the air. I was able to park right at the shop, which was on the first floor of a three-story apartment. The houses on the block were bright blues, greens, and pinks. I grabbed my wallet and was just about to get out of my car when I realized something that I hadn't noticed the week before. I'd been so distracted that I didn't even realize that I was right by my old best friends' cribs. I knew they were around there somewhere. I looked around and found their blue and yellow houses right next to each other. I remember the way we would bust a whole mission just to hang out during the weekend.

* * *

MAY 2015

I was about to be done with my freshman year, and I had been best friends with Valeria Luna and Edwin Rosales since my first day of high school. We met each other during lunch despite them being in the grade above me. They had grown up next door to each other their entire lives, so they were already best friends. We all just clicked with each other.

One Saturday morning, I took the red line and then the pink line to go visit them. As soon as I knocked on Valeria's door, she opened it, smiling.

"Hey, Valeria."

She hugged me and looked down at her phone for the time. "Hey, Ray baby, you made it! It's barely eleven though, so knowing Edwin, he's probably still sleeping. But it's okay. We can hang out in the backyard 'til he wakes up." She gestured for me to follow her through the hallway that led us through her house.

"Alright, that works for me."

She lived in the blue house and inside it, her walls were decorated with religious symbols and family pictures. Her backyard used to be my favorite place because she had a big enough hammock for two people. We would just sit there and talk for hours.

We went to her hammock that day. It was warm out, and the sun seemed to be glowing on her. She had her long, curly hair in a braid down her back. She was about five-foot-five, had these big, light brown eyes, and her long lashes faced the sky. I couldn't figure out what it was about that day specifically, but she somehow looked more beautiful than ever before.

It's not like the thought had never crossed my mind, but I didn't ever let myself take my thoughts seriously. Valeria lived her life with no care in the world but the present. Her peace of mind was what I hoped to reach. She knew how to make you feel alive, and her energy was magnetic.

She had recently started to smoke weed and had gotten me and Edwin onto it. Her parents were always working, especially on the weekends, so whenever we wanted to smoke, we'd go to her backyard. Valeria was everything my parents always told me not to fall for in a girl.

We'd been talking for a while about nothing in particular and passing a joint when she tapped my leg to get my attention and said, "You know what I'm tired of?"

"What, Valeria?" I asked while trying to figure out how I hadn't noticed how cute her dimples were before.

She let out a cloud of smoke into the air and softly groaned, "I'm just so tired of everything being so damn serious. At school, all they do is breathe down our necks about college. We still got three years left. Like, what they so worried about? In this damn house, my mom won't stop coming at me 'cause I haven't gotten a job for the summer yet. Somebody gonna have to tell her it's still illegal for me to work so she can chill. Ray baby, I'm just tryna have fun this summer. You feel me?"

She turned to face me and just smiled. Her eyes were getting red and her pupils were getting smaller, but she still looked just as pretty.

She always called me Ray baby. Said she liked the way it sounded. "I feel you. I'm probably gonna volunteer at the library this summer, though."

Her eyes grew sad, and she looked up at the clouds. "Yeah, programs like that don't really exist out here, and even if they did, I know my mom would beat my ass if she found out I was in one."

I looked at her and tried to read her fake calm composure. "What do you mean, your mom would get mad?"

She put out the joint on the ground. "She'd tell me reading and fun are not for the poor. She hates catching me reading or doing anything that's not cooking or cleaning. That's why I gotta go next door to Edwin's to do my homework. On the weekends, it's easier since my parents aren't around, though."

"I'm sorry, Vale, but I mean, even if we don't volunteer together, we'll still see each other on the weekends."

She looked back up, smiled at the sky, and moved closer to me. She rested her head on my shoulder. "Life would be easier if I could just stay high here with you. Doesn't that sound good?"

My heart was beating out of my chest I didn't know why her touch was making me so nervous. It never had before. All I could think about was how she said she wanted to be next to me. "Yeah, honestly."

She probably wasn't even listening to me then. She never cared about anything but what was going to make her happy at the moment. "I just wish everyone would let me have fun like you do. Like this, baby."

That's the last thing she said to me before she put her hand on my cheek and pulled me in to meet her lips. At first, it was just one long kiss. She tasted like her strawberry Chapstick and weed. But then she kept guiding me with her hands on her face, and we were making out for a couple minutes before she pulled back.

We laid side by side again on the hammock just staring off into the trees and letting the sun burn us for a couple moments. Eventually, I said, "Wow, you know that was my first kiss?" I couldn't believe I could say something as lame as that.

She giggled. "Really? I couldn't tell. But, you see, I just wanna have fun like that this summer. Wasn't that fun?"

"Yeah, I mean, of course, I had fun."

She looked down at her phone and saw a message from Edwin saying he'd just gotten up and that he'd come join us in ten minutes. She said with a smirk, "Okay, well, if we both had fun, let's keep doing it."

"What about Edwin?"

"What do you mean what about Edwin?" She scrunched her face.

"Won't it be awkward if we start doing this?"

"Why would it be awkward if we're all still friends?"

She was the first pretty girl to give me that type of attention, so how could I say no to her? Valeria had a way of making everything sound so easy. "Yeah, let's wait to tell him."

"Okay, Ray baby, sounds good to me."

* * *

JUNE 2019

I walked in to see the same friendly salesman who helped me out last time polishing jewelry.

"Hello, sir, I came in last week and bought the purple-blue ring. Is it ready to be picked up?"

"Yes, son. It's right here. It turned out beautiful, if you ask me. Must be for a real special lady?" He handed me the ring with a box and a bag to put it in.

He was right. The ring looked so good, and Serenity was the most special woman I had ever met. "Yeah, she's special, alright. It's perfect. Thank you so much, sir. Have a good day!"

"Alright now, you have a good day, too," he said. With that, I was out the door. I was about to get back into my car when I heard my name called from down the block. I turned around and saw Edwin with the same friends who had ended our friendship all those years ago.

* * *

SEPTEMBER 2015

Valeria and I spent the entire summer meeting up anytime and anywhere we could. While we were busy fooling around, Edwin was making some new friends from his neighborhood. Since they were next-door neighbors, Valeria was the first to know that he was getting involved with gangs. That's what had me the most fucked up about her. If something was going to ruin her good time, Valeria wasn't going to address it unless someone else brought it up. So, after like a week straight of coming over to her house and not seeing Edwin, I started to get worried. Valeria had twenty different excuses each day, but I finally stopped believing her. The Friday before classes started up again, Edwin wasn't messaging us back.

We were on her bed when I pushed her off me and said "Vale, be honest with me, where the hell is Edwin?"

She looked tired of the question and rolled her eyes at me. "He's with some guys from the block. The ones he's been chilling with all summer. It's all good."

She started to play with my hair, but I just pushed her hand away. "No, Vale, it's not all good. I know those guys are into shady shit. Why would he be hanging out with them?"

She got up, clearly mad, and sat on the opposite side of the bed as far from me as possible. "Damn, Ray, you want me to spell it out for you! He got jumped in, that's why he stays spending time with them."

I felt so hot I thought actual steam might come out both of my ears like in those cartoons. I was mad at myself, too, but I found it easier to yell at Valeria.

"So, you don't give a fuck about Edwin anymore, just cause we're fucking. Nah, Vale, that's messed up."

She got up from the bed and got all up on my face. She yelled back, "You know what, Ray, you're a real dick for saying that. Of course, I care about him, but him joining the gang ain't even that deep. He asked what I thought before he did it, and I told him to go for it."

"Why the fuck would you tell him to do that?" I felt my fists clench. I wanted to punch a wall really badly. More than anything, I wanted to find Edwin.

Her face was red. I could feel her anger, but it just made me angrier. I couldn't understand what she was mad about.

"Ray, not everyone loves school as much as you and got it easy over there in the northside volunteering at the library for fun, okay? This way he's part of them. He'll protect his family and mine too."

She'd been so selfish. "He's gotta undo it, Vale. You gotta convince him to get out. You should've told me. You had so much time to tell me!"

She started crying, and it took everything in me not to run to her to dry her tears and hold her. "You asking for the impossible, Ray. That's not how it works. Once he's in, he's in for life."

"We've been together almost every single day this summer. You could've mentioned it at any time. Do you even care about me, Vale?"

She took a deep breath and wiped away her own tears. "Of course, I love you, but in the same way I did before we started all this. I'm not gonna fall in love with you."

She broke my heart twice in the span of ten minutes. First, she tells me that our best friend is in a gang at age sixteen and then she tells me I had fallen that entire summer for a girl who was never mine to begin with. All I was able to spit out was, "I can't do this anymore—none of it. I can't forgive you for letting Edwin do that. This was the last time, Vale."

She was my first everything, and I believed a part of me would always love her, even if I shouldn't.

I grabbed my wallet and keys and went to her front door. I didn't want to risk her seeing me cry. I had to make Edwin my focus now.

"Raymond, come back. You shouldn't leave like this." That was last thing I heard her say before I was out the door.

The evening was humid and hot. The sun was about to set, and the sky was a blend of orange and light pink. I went straight to Edwin's yellow house next door to have a conversation about everything. I swallowed back my tears and knocked on the door. Laura, one of his four little sisters, answered the door and went to go get him.

"Yo, Raymond, man, you look like shit. What the fuck?" he said as he came out. We sat on his porch steps 'cause the sun was setting soon, and the Chicago summer heat was too much to handle inside the house.

I decided to be completely honest with him. "Yeah, I feel like shit too, Edwin. Valeria just broke my heart, man."

He looked down at his feet for a while and then said, "I know you thought she hadn't told me nothing, but she did a while back. She made it seem like y'all were just fucking, though, no feelings involved."

I looked at the street below where a couple of kids were kicking a soccer ball around. They only stopped for the occasional car that would drive by. "I mean, yeah, she obviously didn't catch feelings, but what can I say? I got attached."

He punched the air a few times. "Raymond, if I knew you loved her for real, I would've told you before. Fuck, I'm sorry, man."

I wondered if this was when he would decide to be honest about the gang, so I said, "What would you have told me?"

"That she broke mine before yours. During the winter, we hooked up, and I told her I wanted to take her on a date. She wasn't having it and said she just wanted us to be best friends who hook up. Join the broken heart club, man."

I could feel myself heating up again at the thought that maybe they had kept on hooking up during the summer. "So, what'd you say?"

He shook his head at the thought. "I told her I didn't want to do that 'cause I'd rather be her best friend than her fuck buddy, so we agreed to pretend it didn't happen. She's bogus for not being honest with you, bro, I'm sorry."

"Wait, so you weren't mad that we've been hooking up even though you loved her before? I would hate me if I were you." I shook my head.

He looked over at Vale's house and couldn't help but smile. "Nah, man. First off, Raymond, you didn't even know. I made the choice to stop looking at her like that. As long as she's happy and safe, I'm happy."

"I think that's what I'd call love then, man—the way you describe her."

"I don't know about that, man. Girls will drive you crazy."

"Yeah, real crazy." I let out a sigh.

"But, man, I heard you been busy. You over there volunteering at the library?"

"Yeah. Gotta get myself set for college."

He rolled his eyes. "You fifteen, Ray."

"Yeah, well—"

Edwin laughed. "That ain't for me." His laugh lost its humor, and then his smile faded altogether. "I quit school."

"What the hell, man?"

"Don't worry, Ray."

But before I could even say a thing, the guys he'd been hanging with all summer stepped outside a house a couple of spots down. I decided to save Valeria and pretend I had no idea who they were.

"Yo, Ed!" one of them yelled.

Edwin waved. "One second," he said to them before turning my way. "I'm good. So, I'm gonna see you tomorrow?"

He knew he wasn't. He knew I couldn't be gang affiliated. We had talked about this at the beginning of the school year. I was serious about getting out of here. So, after breaking up with one of my best friends, and now staring at the other, I lied, "Yeah, man."

That was the last time I spoke to either of them. With that, I went down their block one last time and hopped on the pink line.

* * *

JUNE 2019

"Ray, what the fuck you doing around my hood? I haven't seen you since I left that bum-ass school four years ago," Edwin said, laughing as he walked over to greet me.

"Edwin, yeah, it's been a long time. What you been up to?" I looked to see for myself how much he had changed since four years ago.

He was a lot taller than before. He had to be around six-foot-two with broad shoulders now. Tattoos ran down his arms and neck, and he sported one teardrop underneath his right eye. He looked a lot more tired than a twenty-year-old should look, and his hair was shorter than before. He still had those same familiar bright green eyes and brown skin. "I'm cooling doing the same shit with the same people. I actually just came from seeing Valeria. What about you, man?"

I couldn't help but look over at Valeria's house and wonder if she saw what was happening. I was relieved she wasn't with Edwin. I hadn't talked to her since the end of that summer even though I'd seen her occasionally at school until we graduated. All I knew for sure was that she hadn't been on my mind since I started dating Serenity.

I said, "Damn, that's good y'all still friends after all this time. I'm here 'cause I got my girl her birthday gift from the pawn shop down the block."

"Of course, man, Vale is my ride or die. Damn, lemme guess. Some jewelry? The guy in that shop got some good deals. Where you taking your girl tonight?"

I laughed at how easy it was to talk to him after so long. "Yeah, I got her a ring. We been together for almost three and a half years now. I ain't taking her anywhere tonight, though. She's throwing a party 'cause it's her eighteenth."

He smiled instantly with his big, familiar smile. "Damn, that's a long time. I'm happy for you man. A party. . . shit, I'd love to be able to turn up with you for old time's sake."

I didn't know what to do. I wanted to invite him and get to know the new him, but I knew Serenity didn't like him based on what I'd told her. I figured he must have changed; it had been four years. So, I said, "Yeah, I'm real happy. You should stop by tonight. It'll be fun. It's out in Bronzeville, so give me your number and I'll send you the addy."

His face immediately lit up, and he said, "Are you for real, man? Say less! We in that bitch. Here's my number." He reached for my phone and gave me his number.

The entire time, all I could think about was the fact he said *we,* and how *we* could mean his gang buddies and even Valeria. Both options were just terrible, and I didn't know what I was going to do if they showed up. I texted Jayden to warn him.

"Yeah, man, I'll see you tonight, alright," I said as I walked to my car and thought of how pissed Serenity would be when I told her the news. I was sure she'd be mad.

"Yeah, don't worry. We'll pull up. I'll let you know when we outside."

With that, I drove away and went to Serenity's crib with the fresh peonies and ring on the passenger seat. I could only hope inviting Edwin wouldn't change her answer when I gave her the promise ring that night.

VI.

EDWIN

"Pretty Life" - Terrell Morris, Free n Losh

it hurts me to know that
that you knew how bright she shines
and you still chose to let her go
you said she was too good
what could that possibly mean?
were you that scared of how she made you feel?
like you were worth everything in the world
most people don't get someone like her in their lifetime
and you let her go.

- ESTHER HUESCAS

A HISTORY

Edwin Rosales was a twenty-year-old gangbanger of the 18th Street *Leyendas*.

It's not like he wanted to end up fighting every other day or finessing his way through life with drugs and parties; he wanted to be a chef. He'd always loved to cook, and he treasured his late grandmother's recipe book. He had dreams of opening up his own restaurant in Little Village and making a name for himself. He wanted to be able to only worry about filing his taxes on time and whether he or his wife would pick up the kids from school.

Valeria was the only person in the world he had told these dreams to, and he promised her that one day he would open that restaurant, marry her, and have kids. One day, they would only have to worry about what to make for dinner, not whether or not there would be enough money for dinner.

Edwin was born and raised in Little Village in Chicago's southside in a small basement apartment to his Mexican mother who was only sixteen when he was born, and his Puerto Rican father who was twenty-three. His father left after six months, so Edwin didn't have any memories of him, although his mom would always say they had the same "stupid face" and how every time she looked at Edwin, it would piss her off.

He met Valeria when they were six years old and her family moved into the house next to his. At that point, Edwin's mother had been dating a successful businessman who was forty years old and had a coke problem. His money allowed them to move up to the first floor of the house. Valeria and Edwin immediately became best friends. She had a lot of cousins living with her, which meant her parents rarely checked on them.

By the time they were ten, the businessman was long gone from his mother's life. He did leave them with a good sum of money to keep her from snitching about their affair to his wife. He also left his mother with a big coke addiction. At home, Edwin constantly avoided her, and Valeria became his escape. The two of them would run off into the park every day and have adventures on the playground for hours. When they were together, they would both forget; Valeria would forget that her gross older cousins would try to touch her, and her parents were never home enough to notice, and Edwin would forget that his mother was slipping away more and more every single day.

When Edwin was fifteen, he realized Valeria was beautiful. It wasn't that he thought she was ugly before; he just finally admitted to himself how much he thought about her—all the time. They were spending a lot of time together, too, because they went to the same high school in the northside of Chicago. He'd wake up to her text messages or calls. At night, she was the last thing on his mind before he'd fall asleep.

In high school, Valeria had become—for a lack of a better description—pretty wild. She would go on dates with the eighteen-year-olds in the neighborhood for rides in their cars and the money they gave her. After the dates, she would always spend the night in Edwin's bedroom. There was never anything sexual about them lying next to each other—it was just their way of sleeping peacefully. The next day, she would use the money that the guys gave her to buy them both food. She'd tell Edwin the crazy stories the guys had told her about being in the gangs and the hits they would do. At first, she told the stories in disgust, but then as time passed, Edwin could tell she was slightly impressed. At this point in their story, they were just best friends.

The promiscuous lifestyles of the gang members soon surrounded Valeria. She was curious about her sexuality but admitted to Edwin that she was scared. They were fifteen when they came up with the clear solution: they'd be each other's firsts. To them, the plan was foolproof. They cared for each other, and they wanted to make sure their first time wasn't scary. So, they did it. After that night, neither of them spoke of it for a long time.

During the summer when they were sixteen years old, Edwin started hanging with the 18th Street *Leyendas* to impress Valeria. They had just ended their sophomore year and had known Raymond for about a year. Being a grade apart didn't keep them from being friends with him. Even though he was a year younger, Raymond was taller than Edwin. He even looked a little older, too. Edwin didn't have his growth spurt until seventeen. Valeria tended to get really flirty with Raymond, especially after Edwin would leave. Edwin thought the best way to impress Valeria was to join a gang, so that's what he did.

By the end of the summer, he had successfully joined the gang and later that year, before winter break, he dropped out of high school as a junior. Raymond stopped being friends with him and Valeria because of the gang, which hurt Edwin a lot more than he'd admit. Edwin felt like Raymond had abandoned them. As a result, Edwin and Valeria grew closer together.

By summer of 2016, they were seventeen. One night, they were hanging out as usual in Edwin's bedroom when things escalated. Before they both knew it, they were kissing, and they didn't stop there. The next morning, things didn't go back to normal; they admitted they loved each other.

They didn't have a normal kind of relationship where two people in love choose to commit to each other. More than anything, they had an unspoken agreement. They loved each other and were there for each other but didn't feel the need to label their relationship. Sometimes they would kiss other people, and sometimes even do more with another person, but they only loved each other. At the end of the day, they would always lay in the same bed, and Valeria would always know how to make Edwin laugh.

PART II

VII.

MARIPOSA

"Special Affair/Curse" - The Internet

perhaps the scariest thing about heartbreak
is that you're never sure if they'll remember you the way
you remember them
if it affected them as much as it did you
the aftermath is the real indication of love
because if they stay on your mind
there's a reason why
you just have to be sure you want to hear the true reason why.

- ESTHER HUESCAS

JUNE 2019

Elijah and Jayden nervously whispered on the couch. I couldn't make out what they said, but Jayden had the little crease that formed in between his eyebrows whenever he was worried, so I could tell it was serious. I decided to press them on it because I couldn't imagine what could possibly have been so wrong.

I went and sat on the couch next to them. My hand accidentally brushed up against Jayden's knee. I was mad at myself for not wanting it to stop there. I wondered how his touch alone could send shivers down my spine. He was such a distraction. "Yo, Elijah, what y'all over here whispering about?"

Jayden opened his mouth to say something, but before he could, Elijah cut him off. "Damn, Mari, you real nosy. Don't worry about it."

Elijah and I would rarely fight for real, and he never snapped at me for just asking a question, so I started getting worried. I guess Jayden could tell because he looked my way and blurted out, "It's Raymond. He's bringing Edwin, and Valeria might end up showing up, too."

It hurt me to realize it was still so easy for us to read each other. I quickly reminded myself that we hadn't even spent a minute alone so far that night, so I doubted we were even good.

Elijah shot Jayden a puzzled look that read, "*Why would you tell her?*"

I responded, "Lemme guess. . . Raymond said to make sure I didn't find out so Serenity would hear it from him?" I shifted nervously at being so close to him.

"Yeah, Mari. You gonna stay quiet, right?"

Jayden was looking at the floor, avoiding eye contact with me. I figured that was my answer: we weren't good.

I turned my focus to Elijah and said, "Yeah, I pinky promise. But you better tell Raymond to hurry back and tell Serenity as soon as he walks in." I held up my little finger for Elijah. Ever since we were little, our pinky promises had always been sacred. We'd never break one.

He interlocked his pinky with mine and as soon as he did, Serenity walked into the living room again. She went around and turned off all the lights and then turned on the LED party lights. For a moment, everything was dark. In that momentary darkness, I realized I had to move on. It had been a year. I couldn't let his presence still affect me this much.

Then, the room turned purple, and I saw Jayden again. I knew it'd be hard, but I wasn't about to look dumb for anyone—even him. I felt dumb enough for losing my virginity to him just to have him leave.

Serenity broke the looming silence in the room by starting the party playlist she had been working on. "Okay, Raymond texted me. He said he's on his way back and that he'll be here in five minutes, so we good. Y'all can stop being all weird now!"

Serenity was happy, and I didn't plan on being the one to ruin her mood. Instead, I went up to her and said, "Alright, you guys heard the birthday girl. Let's start the night right with a shot of tequila!"

Serenity had a huge smile on her face as she went to the kitchen to get us cups and bring over the bottle of Don Julio to the living room. She handed us the cups and said, "Mari's got the spirit! Here, guys, drink up."

We all held the red solo cups up into the air to toast Serenity when Raymond walked in through her front door with eighteen peonies in his hands.

Serenity's eyes lit up as soon as she saw him and the flowers. She damn near ran to the door to kiss his cheek. He handed her the peonies. "This is only half of the present. For now, happy birthday, love."

Her smile made her glow. "Raymond, I love them. Thank you. Why'd you take so long, though?" She went to put the flowers in her room so no one would hurt them during the party. Raymond followed her into the room and closed the door behind them. I was glad Raymond was going to be honest with Serenity.

Elijah sighed in relief, and then his phone rang. He turned to us. "I'm gonna answer this call real quick. I'll be back in a few."

With that, Elijah went onto the back porch and took the call in the yard. I wondered if it was one of those girls he'd be going out with and whether or not she'd be at the party. I decided to let him have his secrecy, mostly because this was the first time Jayden and I were alone and at the moment, I was more curious about where that was going to go. Then, I wondered if that made me a shitty sister.

As soon as we heard the back door close, Jayden pulled me closer to him on the couch so that I could hear his low whisper. "Mari, I need to tell you something."

I was confused but whispered back, "Yeah, okay. Is something wrong?"

He looked at me with his big light brown eyes, but it was hard to keep the eye contact going. A few seconds of silence passed until he said, "I never meant to hurt you."

By hurting me, Jayden meant him cutting me off right before he started college last year. The problem was the way he brought it up and how he didn't even try. We were in the same city, after all. I didn't understand what he was feeling because I really didn't see it coming.

* * *

AUGUST 2018

We had hung out all day in downtown Chicago and had made it onto the steps at North Avenue Beach to watch the sunset. Lake Michigan had always brought me peace. Summertime in Chicago was unbeatable.

The skies could have been painted; it looked like cotton candy met the water on the horizon. The moon was also visible that night, bright and almost full.

I couldn't believe the summer was coming to an end, and as if he could read my mind, Jayden held my hand and asked, "What's on your pretty mind?"

I was trying to figure out the best way to say what was actually bothering me and decided to be honest. "I'm thinking it's time to tell our friends what we've been doing. It feels wrong lying to them, especially to my brother."

He looked into the water ahead as if he was searching for the right answer. The silence was killing me. He didn't say anything for what seemed like forever. I was about ready to get my stuff and leave on my own.

"Mariposa, I don't think that's a good idea."

That's all he fucking said. I chose to stay quiet in order to give him a hint that he needed to say more to get a response out of me.

"I don't think this is gonna work," Jayden said.

I didn't want to face his words. I just wanted to jump into the lake and swim away without looking back. I felt like running to the train and going home. Going anywhere but where I was, anywhere but where I had to respond.

I wanted to be his everything so badly. I wanted him to choose me. I wanted him to fight for me. My mind was a mess, coming up with different things to say to get him to change his mind. More than anything, I wanted him to stay. I wondered if giving him something he hadn't had before would be good enough.

I wondered if my body would be good enough.

So, I just kissed him.

It didn't make sense, but for us, it became our way of ignoring difficult questions. Throughout the summer, we'd made our bodies a distraction for all the questions about our relationship that had come up. But we hadn't had sex yet, not that I hadn't wanted to. I was just waiting until we told our friends that we were dating. We'd decided without talking about it that there was no point in ruining the present with problems that could be answered in the future. After all, I heard there was no point in fixing something that wasn't broken. But the summer was ending, so that meant this was the last night that we could pull some dumb shit like we did.

It began to escalate. We were in public, though, so we went to Jayden's car and drove back to my house where—luckily for us—no one was home, not even Elijah. Not one word that left our mouths had to do with anything but what was happening in the moment.

As soon as we made it into the door, we ran up the stairs and went into my room. Once inside, I plugged in my fairy lights that hung up along my walls and turned on my R&B playlist. We took turns freshening up in the bathroom.

When I walked into my bedroom, I saw Jayden had lit up the candles on my desk. He was sitting on the bed with a shy smile as he waited. We started kissing again, but for longer and with more urgency than before. Our clothes quickly ended up on my bedroom floor. The smell of vanilla filled the air. He hesitantly ran his hands over my entire body as if he was exploring it for the first time. He was not a virgin.

Between heavy breaths, I asked, "Do you have a condom?"

Jayden had a puzzled look on his face as he answered. "Yeah, I do. But you sure, Mari? We don't have to."

He looked absolutely perfect to me with his gold necklace shining against his brown skin. He had his hair kind of messed up already, but it somehow made me more attracted to him. In simpler words, he'd never looked better. But, for me, that was not enough to want to have sex. I knew he would be my first love long before that night. That love was more than enough for me. "Yes, I'm sure."

Twenty minutes later, we were laying on my bed next to each other. I kept on starting up little make-out sessions because I knew there was a serious conversation to be had. I was also trying to convince myself that what I had just done wasn't that big of a deal. It was nice being so close to him, and I didn't want the moment to end.

I wanted so badly to run into the bathroom and call Serenity up to tell her everything.

Jayden pulled back and kissed my forehead softly and said in a whisper almost like a secret, "I love you, Mariposa."

I didn't know how much I believed that he really loved me, but in that moment, I found myself not really caring. I just wanted to be honest. I whispered back, "I love you, too."

His pretty light brown eyes looked straight into mine. "I should leave. It's about to be ten, and I'm not tryna push our luck and have your parents or Elijah come back home."

He got up and started getting ready to leave, his eyes scanning my floor for his clothes. I wanted to tell him to stay. Instead, I agreed. "Yeah, you're right."

A small crease formed in between his eyebrows; something was bothering him. But he walked back to my bed and kissed me softly. He reached my bedroom door. "Goodnight, Mari."

"Goodnight, text me when you get home."

I looked on to the street down from my bedroom window to make sure he left safely. Fifteen minutes later, I got his message saying he was home, so I loved the message and went to sleep. We didn't even have a conversation ending it, I was convinced my plan had worked. I was so sure I would wake up to a text from him with plans for the day.

After all, I loved this boy, and he loved me. Damn.

VIII.

SERENITY

"Roll Thru" - Linda Sol, Clarissa Carter

in love we not only learn about ourselves
but of the person we had the privilege to fall for
oh, how easy it is to forget
how lucky we are to be able to experience
everything that is love.

- ESTHER HUESCAS

JUNE 2019

I closed the door behind Raymond as soon as we got inside my bedroom. He hadn't said much to me since he came back, and when he gave me my gift, he was avoiding my eyes. I put down the eighteen peonies on my bed and turned to face him.

"Okay, Raymond. What's going on?" I asked. "Why you acting so weird?"

He jumped onto my bed. I made sure to stand right in front of him so he couldn't keep avoiding me.

"I saw Edwin today," Raymond blurted out. "Valeria wasn't there though."

He said Valeria a lot quieter than Edwin. I was never really the jealous type because I didn't feel insecure, and Raymond never gave me a reason not to trust him. Valeria though. . . The thought of her always pissed me off. She broke Raymond's heart; heartbreak wasn't easy to forget.

I was confused, though, about where, why, and how he saw Edwin. More importantly, I wanted him to answer one thing. "Why you bringing this up?"

He tensed up. "I'm bringing it up 'cause you're my girlfriend. I'mma be honest with you."

"I appreciate that but, Raymond, you tryna tell me nothing else happened besides seeing him?"

"Yeah, alright, Serenity." He let out a sigh. "It's just. . . you know how I hadn't seen him in a minute?"

I hesitated. "Yeah, I know."

"Well, he saw me after I bought your gift and he asked who it was for. I ended up telling him about you and about your party." As soon as he said that, his eyes widened, and he started fumbling with his coat pocket.

"I just think it's funny how you gonna invite them to a party that's supposed to be for my birthday. Raymond, you mean to tell me that you don't see nothing wrong with inviting a gang member and his girlfriend to the party tonight? A girlfriend who you used to fuck with." Wow, I didn't realize how upset he'd made me until then.

"I'm sorry, Serenity. But there's gonna be so many people at the party there's no way they'll be able to ruin anything. I don't want to be on bad terms with Edwin forever. He used to be my best friend." I saw a crease form between his eyebrows. "Is it crazy for me to hope that he'll see all we're doing with our lives and school, and he'll want that for himself, too?"

I hugged Raymond and tried to reassure him that he wasn't crazy for wanting to help his old friend out. The only thing on my mind was making sure Valeria didn't try anything slick at the party.

After letting him get that all out, I said, "No, you're not crazy, love." I kissed him softly on his lips. "I overreacted. I ain't worried about it, okay?"

He kissed my forehead. "Okay. I love you, Serenity."

"I love you too, you goof." I tried to say it with the biggest smile I could give him because I meant every single word. He was my first everything; he taught me what it really meant to love someone. I don't think anyone could've prepared me for the way it feels to be in love with someone. It's deafening, it's blinding, and damn, it's euphoric.

He pulled out a box with a red bow on it from the pocket he had been fidgeting with.

"Serenity, I mean I love you with everything in me. You're the woman of my dreams, but more importantly, you're my best friend." He sat up straighter and with his empty hand he took my right hand. "I have something really important to tell you before I give you your birthday gift."

I felt as if my chest was about to burst, but I gave his hand a little squeeze to calm his nerves. "What is it, love?"

"I got an email saying they made a decision on my NYU application. I wanted to wait to open it with you, Serenity."

I probably wanted Raymond to get into NYU even more than he wanted to. After I got into Columbia for their writing program, I felt as if I was living in a dream. It was my dream, but it didn't make the thought of moving to a new city any less terrifying. I had only known Chicago my entire life;

everyone I loved was here. I didn't even know how to start to let go of that love. You think someone would have taught me how to do that before graduating.

Any part of me that was still upset with Raymond for his secrecy was replaced with attentiveness as he opened the email and got ready to click the 'View update,' that lit up his phone. I grabbed his free hand and squeezed it softly. I swear it was so silent in my room you could hear our hearts beating, threatening to jump out of our chests.

"Open it when you're ready, Raymond."

He clicked the post, and seconds later, purple confetti flew across his screen.

His face lit up, and I screamed with happiness, "Raymond, you got in!"

He hugged me and started tearing up. "Wow, so New York, huh?"

"Yes, New York, together." I hugged him back tightly.

He let me go and placed the small box in my hands. "Happy birthday, Serenity, I hope you like it." He only met my eyes for a second before he looked down at our feet.

I opened the box, and it was the most beautiful ring I had ever seen. The purple-blue gem sparkled even more as I looked at it. "It's beautiful, Raymond! Thank you." I kissed him softly.

He took the ring and put it on my right-hand ring finger, "I can't wait to spend tonight with you."

I caught a glimpse of the time on the clock on my nightstand. We only had five minutes before the party officially started. "Yeah, we should go back and start this party right."

"Yeah, let's go."

We made our way down my hallway. Just before I reached the living room, I saw Jayden and Mariposa kissing on the couch. Without even thinking, I turned to Raymond, who was in awe behind me. I couldn't help but smile, but I signaled for him to not say anything. Instead, I stepped hard so they could hear us.

"Raymond has good news, guys! We gonna be celebrating a lot of things tonight," I screamed loudly to warn them we were coming. By the time we got into the room, Jayden and Mariposa were on opposite sides of the couch. Both pretended as if nothing had happened.

They got up and walked over to the kitchen with us, avoiding getting in each other's way. Elijah came down the hall, and the five of us stood around the kitchen island filled with liquor, pop, and hella cups.

"What's the big news, man?" asked Elijah as he put his arm around Raymond to give him a quick side hug.

"Yeah, what's up, big man?" asked Mari with a huge grin on her face.

"I just found out I got into NYU. I'm going to New York!"

Jayden and Elijah immediately started cheering Raymond on and jumping with him in excitement.

As soon as they broke up their little victory huddle, Mari went to give him a big hug. "I'm so proud of you, Raymond. I told you you'd get in."

"Thank you, Mari, I appreciate it a lot. Don't worry, I'mma look after your girl." Raymond nodded his head in my direction.

Mariposa then turned to me. "You probably real excited, huh? I'm so happy for you, Serenity." She then caught a glimpse of my ring, and her eyes widened. She asked, "That's Raymond's birthday gift to you, right?"

"Yeah, it's really pretty," I said, distracted, as I tried to figure out when I should ask her about Jayden.

"Yeah, it's so beautiful. He asked for your ring size like a month ago, but I never imagined it would be this nice. He did good," she said proudly with a smile.

I wondered what Mariposa was feeling and whether tonight was the first time she and Jayden had kissed. But, more importantly, I wondered if it *wasn't* the first time why hadn't Mari said something to me? I was supposed to be her best friend.

I looked down at my ring, and I couldn't help but wonder when I had stopped being able to read Mari.

IX.

JAYDEN

"Gonna Love Me" - Teyana Taylor

the best conversations are between two people who share
a past
they bounce around subjects
and ask pointless questions
until ultimately it clicks and suddenly it's easy
almost as if they hadn't broken each other's hearts
but not quite.

- ESTHER HUESCAS

JUNE 2019

Mari looked so good. Her slick, long, dark brown hair fell perfectly down her back. She'd been ignoring me the whole night, and I honestly probably deserved it. We had sex last August, and that was the last time we'd hung out alone. I didn't message her or call her with any explanation. It seemed easier to pretend nothing had happened between us instead of telling her the truth: that I was scared of what I was feeling. I was terrified of being in love with her.

I was a mess. I'd wondered what would happen if we started dating and then I fucked it all up. What if she realized she deserved better than me and I lost my best friend? Those fears kept me from loving her out loud, but they didn't stop me from wanting her. I just knew I'd be a mess if she moved on.

I learned that not talking to Mariposa didn't make my love for her go away. It just felt like my feelings were going away because I didn't let myself see her as an option.

I didn't want to keep making the same mistake. So, I decided that night before the party on Serenity's dark blue couch I had to do or say something to win her back. I didn't know where to start, so I just apologized. "I miss you, Mari. I never meant to hurt you."

Mariposa didn't settle for that though. "What you really apologizing for, Jayden?"

I looked her straight in the eyes because I knew that even if my words came out wrong at least she could try to see my truth in the way that I looked at her. I had to be honest. "You deserved better, Mari. You deserved for me to tell you why I couldn't date you."

She looked around before fixing her confused eyes on her shiny silver heels. "Why'd you do it?"

"I wasn't the person you deserved back then. I was going away to college and I didn't want to lose my best friend. I didn't want to hurt you." I paused, then added, "But I know I did."

As she looked up, her eyes were watery, but her voice was strong. "That's not good enough. That's just a shitty excuse, Jayden."

I knew I couldn't hold back this time. It wasn't going to get me anywhere. "I was terrified to love you, Mariposa."

Her eyes lit up as if she didn't expect me to ever admit again that I loved her.

"I'm still terrified," I muttered under my breath.

"What does that mean? I haven't even told anyone about us. I'm over the mind games. What is it that you want?"

I didn't know what I wanted because I'd never had a good example of love. What I learned to call love was my parents' toxic relationship. My father was a functional alcoholic when I was growing up. He always won my mother's forgiveness with roses and promises of sobriety and change the morning after yelling at her. I'd never forget my earliest memory of when I first noticed that shit.

I knew I didn't want to be him. I feared that I hurt Mariposa the way I swore I would never hurt a woman. I had never hit her or yelled at her, but I still made her cry.

Could I have been worse? I let her believe I didn't love her when love was all I felt for her. I felt like I had a better chance of building a time machine and undoing everything than being able to explain it all to Mari.

How could I tell her that the real reason I stopped talking to her was that my father came into the house asking for money. What were the chances that the day after I told her I loved her, life brought back my biggest reason for not believing in it? I'd only seen him a couple of times in the last ten years, and all I saw in him was everything I didn't want to be.

* * *

SEPTEMBER 2018: THE MORNING AFTER

I couldn't believe it. I had finally gotten with the girl of my dreams. I couldn't believe that I finally had told her I loved her.

I woke up confused as I wondered if I should just hurry up and tell our friends about us so I could finally be with her. My mind raced with the possibilities of how the conversations would go. My biggest worry was Elijah.

My mother's yelling interrupted my thoughts. "Omar, what the fuck are you doing here? I don't want the kids to see you like this!"

I immediately ran to the door. I stopped at the end of the hallway so I could hear them more clearly without them seeing me.

My father's thick, husky voice lingered in the air. "Watch how you talk to me, Ana. I ain't one of your little friends."

"No, you need to watch yourself, Omar. You can't walk up in my house asking for shit whenever you feel like it." Her voice was steady and angry.

His voice only got louder. I knew it was only a matter of time before my younger sisters, Leyla and Yomaira, woke up. "Where's the money? I'm the man of the house. Don't forget that."

My sisters' room opened up at the end of the hallway. Yomaira poked her head out a bit and whispered with fear in her eyes, "What's happening?"

I never wanted them to have to grow up as quickly as I had to. I knew the pain in having to hear nothing but yells between people who were supposed to love each other unconditionally. I whispered back, "Stay in your room."

She'd usually put up a fight or make a snarky comment about how I wasn't the boss of her, but this time she went back inside and softly closed the door behind her.

"You a sorry excuse for a man! You left my money the day you left me. I should sue your sorry ass for child support." Her voice sounded tired and rehearsed.

I heard a loud slap.

Before I could hear my mother crying, I knew what he had done. I ran toward my father and lost control. I only saw red.

"Get out! Get the fuck out!"

His cruel deep laugh echoed in my head. "You think I'm gonna let my son talk to me like this?" It was a question, but he meant it more like a warning. I was taller by a couple of inches, so I looked down at him.

His height didn't stop me from feeling small in his presence. His features strikingly reminded me of my own. He had black curly hair and strong, dark eyebrows. His eyes were light brown, which somehow looked angry.

When I looked at him, I reverted back to the scared little boy I was the night he beat my mother and left us for what he claimed was for good.

"Fuck you!" Fighting every tear to appear emotionless, I looked down on him.

He clenched his fist and turned his focus on my mother. "Get your worthless son out of here before I teach him what respect feels like."

My mother went into her purse as more tears fell down her face. She seemed tired of this routine. Like always, she gave in to him and handed him three twenty-dollar bills.

"Here, leave us. We're going to scare the girls if we don't quiet down."

I wanted to scream and tell her that he was just going to keep coming back for the money if she didn't stop. I think deep down, she knew that. She didn't want him to run out of reasons for needing to come to her at least once in a while.

He yanked the bills from my mother's hand and gave me a stupid cocky smile. "You looking good like your father, kid." He must have known those were the last words I wanted to hear, which is probably exactly why he chose to say them.

Quietly, like reciting a prayer, I said, "I am nothing like you."

He laughed in my face. "You have more me in you than you realize."

He left, and my mother locked the door behind him. She held on to me as she cried into my shirt.

I wanted to tell her it was going to be okay. I wanted to reassure her that we'd seen the last of him. I chose to just let the silence talk. I was left wondering how right he was. What were the chances I'd turn out exactly like him? I looked down and saw my mother, broken. I couldn't help but see Mariposa in her. I didn't know what I would do with myself if I was ever the reason behind her tears.

* * *

JUNE 2019

I didn't know how to tell Mariposa that shit had left me fucked up. Instead, I simply said, "I want *you*." I grabbed her chin so she was facing me. I looked down at her lips and then up to meet her eyes before I just said fuck it and went for it. I kissed her, and it felt so easy. I missed running my hands through her hair. She only pulled me closer.

After a while though, she pushed me back, and we sat there smiling at each other like a pair of idiots. She looked perfect.

She then looked at me seriously. "I miss you too, but you gotta show me you ready. This isn't enough." She paused before she added, "Not enough to make up for leaving me without my best friend."

I knew she was right, but before I could say anything, we heard Serenity shouting from the hall. I quickly squeezed her hand and nodded.

Mariposa gave me a small smile before we got up to join Serenity, Raymond, and Elijah in the kitchen.

Raymond shot me a confused look as soon as we made eye contact, but I didn't think anything of it. I was completely distracted, thinking of what I could do to show Mariposa I was different this time. I also needed to prove to myself that being my father's son didn't mean I was my father.

X.

ELIJAH

"Misunderstood" - Lucky Daye

you're all I desire
your touch, your love
the electricity between us is something I have never seen
before
much less felt before
and all I can pray for is please
don't leave me just yet.

- ESTHER HUESCAS

JUNE 2019

I left Jayden and Mariposa alone on the couch. I could pretend that I did it to finally force them to talk and that it was just me being a good brother, but I'd be lying. I left to talk to Diego. It just so happened that I had maybe given Jayden the chance to stop making Mari so sad all the time. I'd convinced myself that as soon as she was honest with me about Jayden, I would be honest with her about being gay and liking Diego.

I'd somehow convinced myself that my lie was okay because I wasn't the only one lying.

I sat on the little bench in Serenity's backyard and answered Diego's call. The summer night sky was a dark blue, and the moon shined bright. Fireflies and pesky mosquitoes filled the sky.

"Hey, are you on your way?" I asked.

"Hi, yeah. I'm like ten minutes out."

I looked over at the door, making sure no one was coming before I said, "Alright. I can't wait to see you."

He laughed. "I'm excited to see you too, but I'm really excited to meet your friends. Especially your sister."

I began to overthink about how I would introduce him and what I would say. Would I say that we were good friends or just friends? Would I say we've hung out a lot outside of practice or lie and say this was the first time? Was Diego expecting me to be more honest about what he meant to me? I honestly hadn't even figured how much he meant to me yet. Relationships were hard enough. My head hurt as I thought of all the added complications of not having come out yet.

But I simply said, "Yeah, me too. I know she'll love you." Oh, shit—love? I hated myself for being so damn intense all the time.

As if he read my thoughts over the phone, he said, "Love, huh?" and laughed. Not in a way where he was making fun of me. It sounded as if he was getting used to the word coming out of my mouth. "I'm sure Mariposa is great, but I'm tryna have you fall in love with me, Elijah, not your twin."

Even though his words made me nervous, he always knew how to make me laugh. It was nervous laughter, but laughter, nonetheless.

I realized that even though it broke my heart a little, I needed to remind him. "I'm sorry I can't present you as more than a friend to them."

"Don't worry," Diego said. "I can be your friend, but not when we're alone."

"Yeah, not when we're alone," I repeated.

Diego sighed softly. "I mean, it hasn't even been a year since I came out to my people. You know most of the team still doesn't even know I'm bisexual."

Diego had a girlfriend until about a year ago. Her name was Alice. They dated for eight months, and she always came to our games. When I started going out with Diego, he told me that he trusted Alice enough to come out to her, but she'd broken up with him because of his sexuality. She didn't want to date someone who was also into guys. She told him it made her feel insecure. Diego ended up taking it as a sign though, and that break up gave him the courage to come out to his family.

* * *

AUGUST 2018

Diego swiped his jersey over his head and used it to wipe the sweat off his face and chest. My eyes were glued on his tan six-pack. The sun loved him. When Diego looked up, our eyes met for a moment. My cheeks burned. I looked away.

Diego laughed. "Come on, Marquez. Race you to the car?"

For a second, I thought he didn't really notice I was staring.

"Or are you gonna stare at me all day?" He smirked and then took off running.

I tried my hardest but was stuck one step behind him the entire time. I didn't mind the view at all.

When I got to the car, I teased, "You cheated, but it's cool, Diego. I guess I'll let you win this one."

"Get in, slowpoke," he said as he unlocked the car. He put on Chapstick before throwing his bag into the backseat. "You wanna throw yours back there too?"

"Yeah, thanks."

Once in the car, he turned his music on and Lucky Daye's "Roll Some Mo," started to play.

"Yo, I fuck with his music," I said, tapping my fingers lightly on the door along to the beat. I looked onto Humboldt Park, which was packed with people playing sports and grilling. I tried to keep myself from wondering how his lips would feel pressed on mine. His arm muscles clenched as he gripped the steering wheel to turn out of the parking lot. It felt wrong having a guy with a girlfriend stuck on my mind. It felt like I was asking to have my heart broken.

"Yeah, he's crazy talented," Diego said, but he sounded distant.

"I haven't seen Alice at the last couple games. How is she?" As soon as the words left my mouth, I hated myself for even asking.

Diego didn't look sad, though, when he said, "I wouldn't know. We broke up a couple weeks ago."

"I'm sorry, man. Y'all was dating for a minute. Are you okay?"

"Yeah, I'm doing alright. She just wasn't the person I was meant to be with." I couldn't help but wonder why he would say *person* instead of girl.

"What happened?"

He looked pensive.

I was definitely overstepping. I always asked too many questions. I just had a gut feeling there was more to the story. "You don't gotta say anything if you don't wanna talk about it, though."

"Nah, don't worry about it. I trust you." He paused. "It's just it's complicated."

We made our way down Humboldt Boulevard, headed to my crib. "What's complicated about it?"

"I told her something about me, and she said she couldn't date me anymore because of it. Honestly, she did me a favor and showed me she didn't like the real me." He nervously tapped his free hand on the top of the steering wheel.

I got nervous and wondered what he had told her and if it was bad enough to not want to know. I teased him, "What'd you do, kill somebody?"

He cracked up and went along with it. "Honestly, she might have liked that better."

I raised my eyebrows slightly and said, "Damn, really? Fuck you do, man?"

"I didn't do anything. It's just who I am that bothered her."

I think at this point he was just trying to figure out how to tell me without saying it out loud. I didn't want to assume was into liked guys, but butterflies flew in my stomach just at the thought. I tried to play it cool. "What do you mean?"

He laughed and rolled his eyes playfully. "I'm bi, Elijah. She didn't like the fact that I also like guys."

Yeah, there it was. My heart started to race as soon as I heard those words come out of his mouth. All I could get out was, "Oh."

I don't think he was expecting me to get so nervous. "Oh, man, is this gonna be a problem?" He was getting upset. "I didn't know you were like that."

I scrambled, trying to figure out the best way to say what I really wanted to say. "No, not a problem. Trust me, I get it."

He raised his eyebrows. "Get it?"

We sat in silence for a little while. We let the soft rumble of the car and music mask the sounds of *elote* vendors and children's laughter before I finally said, "Yeah, Diego, 'cause I'm gay."

Diego's smile lit up the whole car as soon as I said that, and he pulled into a parking spot next to Koz Park. He put the car in park and turned to me. "Oh, shit! You for real?"

"Yeah, I wouldn't lie about something like this." I laughed softly, trying to lighten the mood.

"Man, well, I feel a lot better about having a crush on you now," he said with his big dorky smile.

This was the first time I had a crush on a guy who wasn't an actor, a fictional character, or a guy I had just met on Tinder. I didn't know what to do, but I did know I wanted to kiss him.

I wondered if I should just go for it. I told myself he had stopped the car for a reason. Our eyes were fixated on each other's lips. I unbuckled my seatbelt. Before I could chicken out, I quickly leaned over the console, grabbed the back of his head, and pulled him closer to me.

He quietly said, "Oh," before our lips locked.

He ran his hands through my hair and down my back. It gave me goosebumps. I pulled back, and the taste of sweet strawberry Chapstick lingered on my lips.

* * *

JUNE 2019

Ever since we kissed in his car last summer, we had been secretly going out after practice to get food or on the weekends.

"Yeah, soon though, Diego. I swear I'm going to tell Mariposa and my family real soon."

"I know. I'm gonna be there really soon. Then I gotta find parking," he said.

"Okay, just knock 'cause no one else has gotten here yet."

"See you soon, Marquez."

"See ya." I hung up.

I met everyone else in the kitchen, and Raymond told us about getting into NYU. I was so happy for him. We all were. I wondered why Jayden and Mariposa weren't standing next to each other. I took it that the conversation couldn't have gone that well.

There was a knock at the door as soon as the five of us finished taking a shot in honor of Raymond.

"It's my friend, Diego. I'll get it," I announced to the group.

"Ooh, Diego! I'm excited to meet him, Elijah. Our first guest," Serenity said with a warm smile on her face.

When I opened the door, Diego looked as good as ever. He wore a light-yellow shirt and white shorts. His wavy hair was pushed back, and the familiar smell of his cologne hit me when he walked past me to get in. "Hey, come in." I stopped myself from hugging him and dapped him up instead. What I really wanted to do was kiss him.

We went to the kitchen where I introduced him. "Guys, this is Diego. We play soccer together." I motioned the group toward Diego. Then I pointed to my friends in order. "Diego, this is Mariposa, Serenity, Jayden, and Raymond, my best friends."

They all said hi and took turns asking him about what high school he went to and where he was going to school in the fall. I think it was pretty clear that I looked flustered because Mari shot me a puzzled look that asked if I was okay. I nodded quickly in her direction and then turned my attention to Serenity, who was already taking Diego to give him a quick tour of her house. As soon as I realized they liked him, I went back to breathing normally.

"Oh, shit, it's happening! People are outside finding parking." Mari smiled as she looked out the window. "You excited, Elijah?"

I snuck a look over at Diego laughing with Serenity. "Yeah, I am."

XI.

RAYMOND

"Sunny Duet" - Noname ft. The Mind

my only advice is
love hard
give it your all
and then some more because without
intensity
there isn't a fear of loss
and without fear,
there can't be love.

- ESTHER HUESCAS

JUNE 2019

I thought Diego seemed pretty cool. Elijah started acting pretty weird as soon as he got here, though. I wondered why.

Serenity was glowing as she brought out the wristbands and set them on the table. "Okay, guys, I'mma put these here and take some so when y'all collect money from people at the door, you can give them a wristband in return." She smiled before adding, "Oh, and obviously take the one that belongs to you and put it on."

"Wait, what do the colors mean?" Jayden asked as he took a couple and put them in his pocket.

"Green is single, yellow is complicated, and red is taken. Real easy," Serenity said but she shot a puzzled look at me. I think it was clear we were both wondering what Jayden and Mari were going to pick.

Serenity handed me a red one and then asked me, "Can you help me put mine on, please?"

"Yeah, of course."

"Oh, okay, I get it. Real smart." Jayden said. He looked over at Mari, as if he was wondering what to do. But before Jayden got the chance to pick, Mari went straight for green and put it on herself.

I thought about how that one must have really hurt him. Jayden looked over at Mari, confused, but it didn't stop him from putting on a yellow one.

Elijah went straight for a green one, and Diego got a yellow one. Elijah didn't say anything about Jayden picking yellow, which made me wonder if Mariposa had told him about Jayden and her. Elijah could have also just been distracted because he was helping Diego put his wristband on.

There was a knock on the door, and Mariposa went over to answer it. She let in ten people from school after they gave her the money for their wristbands.

While everyone was distracted and busy getting drunk, I told Jayden we needed to talk. I took him to the living room corner farthest from the kitchen.

I pointed at his wrist and said, "So, yellow, huh? You tryna tell me who got you confused? Or if you want, I could guess?"

He laughed and said, "Nah, man. It's nothing yet. Just a girl that I'm not tryna mess things up with by getting with someone else tonight."

"Yeah, Mariposa is great. I agree with you, you shouldn't want to fuck that up."

His eyebrow raised. "She told you?"

"Nah, man, Serenity and I saw y'all kiss on her couch earlier." I wanted to know how he was really feeling, though, so I added, "But since you grabbed yellow, I'm guessing y'all have done more than just kiss tonight."

"Damn, I can't believe I didn't hear y'all. You could be a spy, man." He laughed. "But, yeah, we were talking last summer, but now I don't know how to fix what I messed up."

"How deep were you?"

"Shit." He paused and lowered his voice. "I'm pretty sure I'm in love with her."

He took me by surprise. "Wait, hold up, man. . . you in love with her?" I knew he must have done something bogus. Mari wasn't the type of person to be mean without a good reason, especially because they had been best friends before whatever happened to them. As soon as they met, they clicked. "You must have made her big mad, then, to get her to pick green tonight."

Across the room, I noticed that Mariposa was talking to a big group of people from our high school. A couple of guys in the group had asked me to put them on with her in the past, but Mari said no every time. From where we were, we could clearly see her smiling big and laughing.

"Yeah, you know how I told you about my dad coming over last September?"

I thought back to how fucked up seeing his dad had got him. He'd spent a lot of time at my house that following week. "Yeah, I remember."

"I let my parents' relationship get in my head and ghosted her. How do I come back from that?" He looked frustrated and kept taking big sips of the tequila in his cup.

"Damn, you gotta realize you're not your dad, Jayden. You also gotta want Mari bad enough, though." I caught a glimpse of Serenity across the room looking stunning and then added, "If I've learned anything from dating Serenity, it's that love is a choice. You gotta put in the work for it to last. Do you want it to last, Jayden?"

"Yes. I needed the last nine months to figure that out, but I'm sure now. I want her."

"Okay, good. Now stop drinking tequila and go get your girl away from those horny-ass boys." I took the empty cup from his hand and put it under my full one.

"Thanks, Raymond." He pointed at the phone in my hand and said, "How about your little problem?" He was referring to Edwin and Valeria, but I was sure he mostly meant Valeria. I tried to tune out my thoughts and let myself feel the vibrations of bass coming from the speaker.

I knew I couldn't keep on putting it off, so I looked down to read the text I'd been ignoring for the past couple minutes. I was afraid of what it would say. It was from Edwin, and it read, "*We parking.*" I showed my phone to Jayden, and we looked around the living room that was already packed with people, some of whom I had never met.

"You think he's in here yet?"

"Maybe. Somebody could've already got their money at the door."

"So, Valeria is gonna come, huh?" Jayden raised his eyebrow at me. "She had you wrapped around her finger back then. Isn't it crazy how time changes everything?"

"Yeah, apparently she's gonna come. I think she's with Edwin now."

"Valeria is lowkey crazy, though. You better be careful. I remember when her and Edwin came over to your house one time and I was there. She was wild."

Crazy? I wondered if I had been really that blind back then. Besides how it ended, I always believed she was a good person.

"I always hoped she'd keep Edwin in check, you know?" I assumed since I saw him that afternoon still messing around with the same type of people, she didn't actually do that. That's honestly what hurt me the most—seeing Edwin all caught up.

"Honestly, I always assumed he'd be the one to keep her out of trouble." I was confused about what Jayden said. I wondered if it was possible that I'd had it wrong back then; maybe Valeria needed guidance, not just Edwin. But before I could ask Jayden what he meant by his comment, I saw her walk in with Edwin by her side.

I knew Edwin had changed, but Valeria looked like a version of herself I didn't imagine she could be. Her face hadn't changed much, and her curly brown hair was loose and fell down her back. She had scattered tattoos that covered parts of her arms. Valeria kissed Edwin on the cheek and pointed to us. He nodded, and she started toward us.

They walked in with two big, broad guys covered in tattoos and wearing all black. The girl with them had long blond hair that stood out against her dark, olive-brown skin.

Edwin had changed to a new and more expensive black outfit than the one he had on earlier that day. He had on a big, shiny watch and a gold chain. He went over to the kitchen to get a drink with the others who came with him.

"Oh, shit," Jayden muttered as he saw Valeria walk toward us.

Her smile seemed familiar, but her words were foreign. "Hey, boys, long time no see." She looked Jayden up and down. "Jayden, you've only gotten finer since the last time I saw you."

I knew I could always count on Valeria to say whatever was on her mind and in the bluntest way possible. Jayden laughed awkwardly. "Nice to see you too, Valeria."

"It's good to see you, Raymond. I just wanted to say thanks for the invite. I also wanted to know where I could find the birthday girl." She looked around the room quickly before she said, "Since Edwin told me he ran into you, I've been real excited to meet the girlfriend."

I was irritated by how she was referencing Serenity. I didn't know what she thought she was going to accomplish talking about her like that. "Her name's Serenity, and she's around here somewhere enjoying her birthday. Maybe you'll get to meet her later."

"No need for the attitude, handsome. I think I already spotted her. I'm gonna take a wild guess and say she's the girl in the tiara. The one next to the girl in the red dress." Valeria pointed directly at Serenity and Mariposa, who were now in the kitchen. "Edwin seems to have already found her. Why don't we go meet with them? Jayden, you should come too. Let's turn that frown upside down and get a couple shots."

The Edwin I knew wouldn't pull anything slick. I just didn't know how much Edwin had changed. I didn't like the idea of his friends being so close to Serenity or Mariposa. I grabbed Jayden by his shoulder and said, "Yeah, sounds like a great idea. Let's go."

Thankfully, Valeria led the way through the sweaty crowd of people in the living room. I was able to whisper to Jayden, "You better not be thinking of drinking more. Focus on your goal."

Jayden looked down at the wristband and said, "Trust me, I'm focused."

PART III

XII.

MARIPOSA

"Do I Make You Nervous" - Serena Isioma

I found myself when I least expected to
with you
I lost myself when I most expected to
with you
I saw our end before I could even fathom our beginning
what a twisted story
it was to fall for you.

- ESTHER HUESCAS

JUNE 2019

The living room was packed with people from all five of our pasts and presents. The room smelled of weed, sweat, and liquor, which pretty much meant it was a successful Chicago house party.

I didn't know what to do. I couldn't believe Jayden had kissed me. I had been waiting for that stupid kiss for the last nine months. I wanted to believe things would be different, but I didn't want to risk looking dumb. All I wanted was to get my best friend's advice.

I somehow had come to the decision that the only way to get Jayden's attention was to piss him off. My dumb-ass plan backfired, and it instead got me stuck talking with the annoying football players from our high school.

Soon enough, the boys got distracted when some girls started to hit on them. Serenity then took me to the side and hit me with, "Were you ever going to tell me about Jayden?"

I nearly choked on the vodka lemonade I was sipping on. "I did want to tell you, Serenity. I just got carried away, I guess." My voice drifted off. I didn't know what to tell her because I didn't have any real excuse besides being embarrassed.

Serenity put her hand on my shoulder. "You could've told me, Mari." She didn't seem mad or even sad, just curious.

I couldn't help but notice Raymond was talking with Jayden across the room. I wondered if it was about us, too. It was shocking how well he and Serenity could play cupid.

"I know. How'd you even find out? Did Jayden tell Raymond?"

She laughed. "Oh, no, Mari. If Raymond would've known before me, I would be really mad right now."

I raised my eyebrow. "So, how?"

"We saw you kiss tonight, silly. With a kiss like that, I knew it couldn't be the first one. I just don't get why you didn't tell me."

I should've known that having kissed Jayden in the living room with all our best friends in the same house probably wasn't the smartest decision if we weren't trying to get caught. I wondered if part of me had let it happen because of the risk. Maybe I'd gotten tired of pretending and just wanted everyone to finally know. I mean, I knew I wanted everyone to know about Jayden, but only as long as there was something to tell. So far, there wasn't anything yet to tell.

I gave Serenity a recap of everything. I told her about last summer, about falling in love, about us having sex, and about Jayden ghosting me after that. "I didn't tell you because I didn't want to cause trouble with all of our friendships," I added because Serenity's facial expression had changed from hurt to anger. She kept flicking hateful looks Jayden's way.

Serenity shook her head in concern and asked, "Is Jayden dumb? He's my friend, but I won't hesitate to tell him off if he tries anything. You can't look dumb just to please him, Mari."

"You right. He needs to show me that he's ready now. Not just by telling me he loves me. I won't let him be with me without committing anymore, Serenity. I'm worth more than being a secret." I hadn't realized that was what I'd been searching for when I was talking to him earlier that night. I wanted a sign of real commitment and no more empty promises. I knew I deserved something that didn't leave me confused and hurt.

"I know you'll figure it out." Serenity paused and quickly looked over at Raymond with a smile. "If I've learned one thing, it's that if someone wants you, best believe they're going to fight like hell to get you."

"Thanks, but I owe you an apology, Serenity. I shouldn't have waited a year to tell you about me and Jayden." I wished I had told her earlier, but more than anything, I really wished that I had been able to tell Elijah first. Even as annoying as my twin brother could be, he was blood, and that always came first.

"No, Mari, I owe you an apology. I haven't been a good friend lately. I love Raymond, but you're my best friend too, and I shouldn't have stopped being able to read you so well. Maybe if I would have been paying more attention, y'all would be dating right now instead of awkwardly looking at each other from across the room. 'Cause don't think that I can't tell you keep moving slightly to make sure you can keep seeing him here, you creep!" She laughed and then went in to hug me.

"I've missed you," I said, hugging her tight before I let go.

"I've missed you too, Mari. But let's stop being so serious. This is a party, after all!"

I grabbed her hand and took her to the kitchen island to get us both another drink. As soon as we finished pouring our drinks, none other than Edwin and Valeria walked into the house with their little group.

Valeria looked amazing. I'd never met her before that night, but I'd seen her pictures on Facebook and had heard enough about her to know to keep my guard up. I noticed Elijah and Diego were at the front door, so they collected their money and gave them their wristbands. Edwin looked exactly how Serenity had described him. He had even bigger muscles and a more intimidating facial expression than I could've imagined.

"I think both of them have grown up a little since I saw their Facebook pictures three years ago," I said as I nodded my head in their direction.

"Wow, yeah. I didn't actually think she'd show up. I mean, why show up to your ex's girlfriend's birthday party? An ex you haven't talked to in years." Serenity rarely got upset, but I could tell that this situation was bothering her. We saw Valeria kiss Edwin on the cheek and then walk over to Raymond and Jayden.

Jayden had told me about the time he met Valeria at Raymond's house back when they were all still friends. Jayden warned me that Valeria always did what she wanted because she treated everything and everyone like a game. He also had explained to me the real reason why Raymond ended up getting hurt. Edwin started walking straight for us in the kitchen. He walked through the crowd like he was the king of the room. I was positive that part of him thought he was, too. I didn't like it.

He came up to us shining a big cocky smile. "Happy Birthday, beautiful. You must be Ray's girl," said Edwin as he poured straight tequila into a cup.

He didn't hesitate as he drank his cup all at once, but Serenity remained cool. "Yeah, that's me, Raymond's girlfriend. My name is Serenity, and you must be Edwin. He mentioned you might come."

I wished I could be as unbothered by him as she seemed. He probably wasn't used to not being treated like a king. I bit my tongue. I didn't want to add to the problem. It was Serenity's big night, anyway.

Edwin looked me up and down before he said, "I don't know who you are, though. But unlike Raymond's Mrs. over here, you're single, right?" He looked down at my wrist with a dumb-ass grin on his face. I beat myself up for being stubborn earlier and not having put on the yellow wristband and making things good with Jayden once and for all. That stupid wristband was just giving me problems.

"My name is Mariposa, and I may be single, but I'm also good." I was so irritated that I let myself roll my eyes at him. I was so distracted I didn't notice Valeria had come up to us with Jayden and Raymond.

"I didn't realize Mexican Barbie had so much attitude," Valeria said as she pointed her long red acrylic nails at me.

"Who do you think you are? You can't just walk up in here and start insulting people," I said as I got closer to her face.

Edwin pulled Valeria back by her arm in an attempt to get her away from me. "It's okay, Vale. We were just getting to know each other." He flashed a grin at me. "You must be confused, Mariposa, 'cause I'm with Valeria. I'm not looking for no one tonight, either."

"See, baby girl? I don't know what kind of fantasy you've created in your head, but my man doesn't want you."

"Yeah, okay."

"We all know I'm far prettier. I mean, it's clear you don't even got a man by your side."

"You know, I was gonna be nice, but actually—" Serenity began to say before Raymond cut her off.

"Yo, Serenity. It's okay." Raymond tried to grab her hand, but she pushed it away.

I decided it wasn't worth it to argue with Valeria and put Serenity in a more difficult position. I'd rather not have to deal with a potentially cheating douche and his possessive girlfriend. "Alright, well, I'm gonna go somewhere else 'cause I don't care enough to entertain an argument with people I just met."

I tried to make eye contact with Serenity, but she was busy trying to subtly get away from Raymond's reach.

I went toward the hallway to go out through the back. Before I got too far, I heard Jayden say, "You haven't grown up at all, Valeria, and it's been three years. You gotta eventually stop acting like you're young and ain't got anything to lose."

When Jayden caught up to me, he smiled, and I immediately felt better.

"Mari, can we go outside to talk? I'm not trying to waste your time."

"Yeah, I'd like that."

I was walking one step in front of him the whole time, until at one point he took my hand and squeezed it gently. When he held my hand, I felt safe.

I opened the door to the yard and stopped dead in my tracks. Elijah was making out with Diego. We startled them, and they immediately stopped. Elijah jumped back. I didn't know what to say. I just stood there, frozen.

My twin brother was into guys, and he hadn't ever told me. I realized I wasn't the only person who had sacrificed their best friends for romance. I knew I had fucked up. Elijah was talking to me but his words didn't make sense. All I said was, "Wow."

Both Elijah's and Diego's faces were bright red. I finally heard Elijah say, "I didn't want you to find out like this. I'm sorry."

Jayden looked confused for a second but soon went over to Elijah and hugged him. "I wish you felt you could've told me, man. I'll support you, always."

This was a mess. Everything had just gotten so complicated tonight. My mind was racing, and I didn't know what to even think. I had a tendency to run, and that is exactly what I did. As I started to run inside to Serenity's room, I heard Elijah shout, "What the fuck, Mari?"

I sat on Serenity's bed and tried to get myself together. I hated myself for not having run to him with open arms.

I heard a knock on the door and Elijah's voice saying, "Mari, I'm coming in."

Before I could say anything, he entered with a red, wet face. We looked at each other in silence.

"You know I love you, right?" I asked.

"Well, that's good. You're stuck with me," Elijah teased. "I love you too, you goof."

My legs were shaking, and I tried to breathe deeply to keep myself calm. "I need you to know that I couldn't care less who you love as long as he treats you right."

"Then why did you storm off, Mari?"

I wanted to tell him that I missed the days when we would tell each other everything. I wanted to ask him if he remembered when things had changed between us. "I wish I could've been the person you trusted with your secret. I just feel like the shittiest sister."

I got up from the bed and walked over to where he was standing by the door. I put my arms around him and squeezed him tight. He held onto me just as tightly. The only sound in the air was muffled music and voices from the living room.

He let me go. "I was scared, Mari. But you not wrong. No more secrets."

I couldn't help but smile as I noticed how Elijah was glowing. Besides the dried tears from our conversation, he was beaming. It was the type of radiance that only comes from knowing you're loved. "Okay, so you and Diego?"

He laughed. "Yeah, he's great. We're actually really serious. He's my boyfriend."

My eyes widened. "Boyfriend?"

"Yeah. I really like him, Mari."

"I'm really happy for you."

Admitting how I felt was not something that came easily to me, even if it was to my twin brother, so I kept it at that. I could've kept going on about how much his happiness meant to me. I could have told him how I would've done anything to see him smile and how I would do anything for him to be loved unconditionally.

"I'm gonna go reassure Diego that my sister isn't a homophobe." Elijah laughed and playfully punched me in my arm.

"Oh, God, please go do that. He's gonna hate me already if you don't tell him."

"Yeah, don't worry. No one could hate you."

We hugged again and left Serenity's room, closing the door behind us. Before we went our separate ways, he said with a wink, "You deserve to be happy, too."

I guessed I probably hadn't been as good at hiding my secret as he had been.

I watched Elijah walk with Diego by his side, a sight I knew I could grow to love.

I went back to the backyard where I found Jayden sitting down on the bench. I took the empty seat next to him.

"Hey." I smiled softly as I fully took in that moment under the summer moonlight.

"Hey." He kissed my forehead gently once I sat down.

It was a good secret while it had lasted.

There wasn't a need for secrets anymore. They no longer seemed worth it.

XIII.

SERENITY

"Lost" - Chance the Rapper, Noname

it's hard to appease everyone
not only hard
but impossible
all we can do is try
try to do the right thing
try to keep around the right people
try to do good
but most importantly
try to be the good.

- ESTHER HUESCAS

JUNE 2019

"Okay, dramatic," Valeria muttered underneath her breath. Mariposa had just stormed off, and Jayden had run after her.

I rolled my eyes, and I wasn't trying to hide it. She didn't say anything, and I took that as a small win. I didn't understand when in the night I had begun to compete with Raymond's ex. Mariposa could stand on her own, and I knew she didn't need me to help defend her. The idea of entertaining Valeria wasn't sitting well with me.

I could feel the bass of the speaker from where we were standing in the kitchen. I focused on the sticky floors instead of Valeria's jealous looks.

Raymond kept trying to hold my hand and get me to look his way, but I was fuming. I didn't understand how he could try to shut me up in front of her. I was angry but trying my hardest not to let it show. I was convinced it would just prove Valeria right.

He seemed to want to make things worse with me. "I think we should all calm down. There's no need to be fighting. It's a party."

"You know how these females are, bro. They love the drama." Edwin dapped him up and put his hand on Raymond's shoulder, guiding him toward the bottles.

Valeria followed his lead and let her hand interlock with Edwin's. She laughed. "Have you ever thought it's the drama that loves me?"

Raymond laughed nervously along with them. I tried my hardest to block out the reality that this was happening on my birthday.

I shouldn't have followed them, but I didn't know where else to go. I couldn't see Elijah and Diego anywhere, and I definitely wasn't about to follow Mari and Jayden. I knew they needed to talk.

My stomach hurt just by looking at the bottles lined up in front of us. Edwin served himself and Valeria a shot of Jose

Cuervo. I'd lost count of how many I'd seen him take since he came. I also wouldn't have been surprised if they had been drinking before they arrived.

Edwin held the bottle over Raymond's cup and asked, "You ready for another one?"

Raymond looked over at me, but I kept my expression blank. He moved his cup away and tried to stand a bit closer to me. "Nah, man. I'm good for now."

"Suit yourself," Edwin said before he cheered Valeria and they took their shots. He let the bitter taste leave his mouth before he asked, "So, Raymond, how you been since high school?"

I wondered if he was asking him simply out of curiosity or if he wanted something else from him. "Really good, actually. I'm going to NYU this fall."

Edwin smiled softly and then quickly went back to his resting "I don't care about anything" face. "Good for you, man."

Valeria smiled and reached for Raymond's hand, but Raymond stepped back to avoid her. She ignored the rejection and said, "I'm proud of you, Ray baby."

I took a step forward, toward her, but Raymond grabbed me around the waist. I let him hold me back. My nostrils flared as I took a deep breath. "Yeah, we'll be together in New York." I returned her snarky smile. "Should be a lot of fun living with my man, soon."

I felt safer with his arms around me.

Raymond smiled. "Serenity is going to Columbia. She's a really talented writer. Y'all will have to keep a look out for her work real soon." I knew he meant it, but somehow it felt as if he was saying it just to say it.

Valeria seemed to be distracted, though, which irritated me because I was trying to very subtly tell her to cut it with the extra friendliness and touchiness with Raymond. She was staring off past me and looking at my front door. Three big guys, all with coordinating purple outfits and thin gold chains, had entered. They had tattoos similar to Edwin's and his friends' down their arms and legs.

They were searching the crowd intensely but hadn't seemed to find who they were looking for yet. I assumed they weren't here to wish me a happy birthday; I'd never seen them before.

Valeria's eyes widened, and she muttered, "Shit." Then, she softly tapped Edwin, who was distracted by his red solo cup, to look up at the guys.

"Man, fuck! What those bitches doing here?" Edwin muttered under his breath.

"You know them, Edwin?" Raymond asked.

"Not really." Edwin called over his friends, who were busy getting drunk and hitting on some of the girls from our school. He said something to them low enough so Raymond and I couldn't hear. Meanwhile, the mystery guys at the door were coming toward us. They had all put on green wristbands.

"Who are those guys, Raymond?" I was getting angrier at everyone, including Raymond, the closer they got.

"Well, fuck," Valeria muttered.

Despite the fact that they wore coordinating fits, they didn't look that similar. There were three of them. One was a tall dark-skinned guy with short hair. The second was a medium-built brown-skinned man with curly hair. He had a big cross tattoo with a rosary that took up his whole neck and seemed to go down his back. The third was a pale, short, big guy with dark black hair in a short buzz cut. Although he was the shortest, he seemed to lead the pack.

The brown-skinned one spoke first. He looked up and down at Valeria before he said, "Yo, mamas, you tryna dance?"

"Nah, I'm good. I don't fuck with opps." She stood up taller and got closer to Edwin.

He laughed. "You must be fucking with a bitch if you think I'm the opp, mamas." He nodded his head slightly toward Edwin. He then put his arm around Valeria's waist and said, "I can show you a real good time. You don't gotta hang with these 18th Street lames anymore." He moved his hand quickly down her back to touch her ass. She tried to jump out of reach but couldn't.

Edwin's face was red. If we were in a cartoon, steam would've poured out of his ears.

Edwin immediately got up in the guy's face. "So, you wanna come over here and disrespect my girl and my family?"

I wondered if by "family" he meant just his friends or the gang as a whole.

"It sounds like y'all want me and my boys to show y'all what the 18th Street *Leyendas* are about. Time you start respecting our name, bitch."

The tall, dark-skinned guy made his way closer to Edwin and said in a low and raspy voice, "We'll be in the front." They laughed and made their way through the crowd out the door. The music was loud enough that not everyone in the room heard the argument, but it did make everyone around us stare.

I looked down and noticed that at some point during the confrontation I'd let myself hold on to Raymond's hand. Now, I didn't want to let go.

Edwin was getting the boys ready, telling them they were going to have to fight when he stopped his ranting to look at

Valeria. "You okay, Vale? I ain't gonna let nobody disrespect you. Especially not those Pulaski Disciples."

Valeria looked tired but kissed him softly on the lips and said, "Yeah, I'm alright, *amor.* Y'all do what you got to do. I'mma go with y'all. I'mma step in if I see them doing any dumb shit."

Edwin smiled softly at her and looked down to meet her eyes. "No, I ain't gonna let you. You stay here with Serenity. I'll be back when we teach them a lesson. Alright?" He then looked at me. "That alright with you, Serenity? You make sure she doesn't go after me. I just don't want my pretty girl getting hit."

He seemed so sincere, yet I was confused about what they meant to each other. They didn't act like boyfriend and girlfriend but simply like they knew no matter what they had each other. I didn't hear any doubt in Edwin's voice when he called her his girl nor in Valeria's when she said she was true to him. I was trying my hardest to normalize the situation, but I couldn't wrap my head around what was happening.

"Yeah, we'll stay with her." I let the words escape my mouth before I said something I knew I'd regret.

"Actually, Raymond, can you come spot me and my boys?" Edwin asked.

"No. He's not going," I immediately said to Edwin. I mean, I was positive he'd never go. It went against the very reason he stopped being friends with Edwin in the first place. He didn't want to get involved with that shit. I didn't expect him to say anything other than "No."

Raymond squeezed my hand gently.

Edwin ignored me. "I don't want you fighting. It's just in case something happens you can come get Valeria, and she'll know what to do. One bad punch, and I gotta get my boys and Vale out before they call more of their friends."

I found it hard to believe he was asking Raymond for help. "Listen, I think it's time you all leave."

"I'm sorry," Raymond started but then turned to me. "Serenity, I'm gonna go help Edwin. I'm just going to make sure nothing real bad happens, okay?"

I couldn't believe him. I'm pretty sure my mouth actually fell open.

I let go of his hand. "No, Raymond. You can't. It's not safe."

"I'm sorry, baby. I have to."

"No, you don't. You should stay here with me."

My face was turning red, and I couldn't stop my eyes from watering. I wasn't about to cry. So, I swallowed back my tears.

Raymond looked me in the eyes and said, "I'm sorry." That was all I got.

I hated myself for feeling the need to say, "If you go with them, Raymond, just know I won't let it go."

"I'm so sorry, Serenity."

I bottled up the million thoughts that ran through my mind.

Edwin whispered something to Valeria that made her smile, and he kissed her forehead quickly. She had been pretty quiet, as if she expected it to happen.

Raymond avoided my eyes and followed Edwin and his friends through the crowd and out the door. Before they opened it, Valeria called out Edwin's name. When he looked back, she made a sign around her heart and mouthed, "*Amor.*"

He smiled. "*Amor.*"

With that, they were all out the door. Elijah and Diego walked up to where Valeria and I were standing.

Elijah said, "How's your birthday going, Serenity?"

I honestly thought this was literally the worst way the night could have gone, but instead of saying all that, I went with the facts. "Oh, fine. It's just my birthday party, and my boyfriend is checking on the gang fight happening in my front yard."

Elijah joined me in my worry. "Raymond's outside? Shit. . . we have to go help or break it off. I don't know. We gotta do something. This ain't right."

All I needed was one person to reassure me I wasn't overreacting. "You right, let's go outside." I turned to look at Valeria, who was nervously looking around until I met her eyes. "Come on, Valeria. We ain't gonna let these boys get hurt."

XIV.

JAYDEN

"Coffee and Cigarettes" - *Vic Mensa*

meant to be
love at first sight
a soul mate
a twin flame
are all ideas that encompass greatness
they all survive on the idea that there's nothing better out there
but sometimes it's okay to still be unsure
to just chase something if it feels right then
after all we're young
there isn't a better time to fall in love.

- ESTHER HUESCAS

JUNE 2019

I couldn't believe that I hadn't known that Elijah was gay. I couldn't help but wonder if I could've said something before that would've made him more open with me.

I heard the music blasting from the inside of the house and the voices of all the people having a good time. Outside in Serenity's backyard, we were far away enough from downtown that some stars shined in the sky. The moon was bright and almost full; it seemed to illuminate Mariposa's face. We were both sitting on the polished wooden bench with enough distance between us to drive me insane. I wondered how two people could be so close physically and yet so far away. She was looking at the sky and concentrating on a plane moving north, toward O'Hare.

I broke the silence. "Do you remember the first day we met, Mari?" I paused and saw she had started to look at me instead of the sky. "You know, at the party Raymond took me to two years ago?"

I was able to get a small smile from her that quickly disappeared. "Yeah, I do."

"Well, what you don't know is that I almost kissed you that night." I really did want to kiss her. Her energy was intoxicating. I loved that she was unpredictable, and that she didn't spend any time that night two years ago on small talk. She acted like she had known me her whole life, and the conversation just kept going. We learned about each other along the way. But I didn't know how to say all that. Not yet.

She looked puzzled. "You're right, I didn't know that. Why?"

The surrounding American elm trees made it feel as if anything that we said was only ours to hear. "Well, for one, you're beautiful," I said. The moon exposed her secret; she blushed. "But that wasn't why I wanted to kiss you. Well, not the whole reason, anyway. It was mostly because you were honest and you made me want to be honest. I'll never forget the random question you asked me."

I laughed, and she joined me. "Yeah, random does sound like me. What did I even ask you, though, that was so unforgettable?"

"You said, 'What's your story?' I remember you said it looked like I had something on my mind, and that's why you even asked me that in the first place. What's honestly crazy is the fact that at the start of the night, I was thinking about my ex Andrea and how she did me dirty. But I swear the moment I saw you I couldn't think of anyone else but you."

A couple of fireflies were flying through the yard. I hoped that the summer night breeze would be strong enough to push us closer together.

"Oh, that question. Well, Jayden, I'm glad you trusted me back then, and. . . I don't know, I guess I'd just never met someone so hurt by love already at that age. I didn't agree with you when you said that love was for fools back then and I still don't to this day." Her voice drifted. She ended up almost whispering, "Regardless of you breaking my heart last year."

I grabbed her hand, cutting the tension built between us. I looked into her brown eyes intently. I didn't want her to think for a second longer that I didn't mean it when I said I was sorry. "I didn't want to hurt you. See, Mari, what I'm tryna say by bringing up our first conversation is that I was scared as fuck to be in a relationship with you. You taught me what love is, and I realized that I hadn't really felt that before. I didn't want to get hurt again. Instead, I just fucked shit up before it even started."

I was rambling, and she could tell. She smiled softly and held a finger to her lips. I only stopped talking to catch my breath. I would've said more. I was getting ready to tell her everything that was going through my mind on my way home after we had sex, but she cut me off.

She sighed and said, "If you live your life in fear, Jayden, you're not allowing yourself to fully feel anything. I think you were so afraid of me hurting you that you hurt yourself instead, and in the process, stopped yourself from being happy." She paused and squeezed my hand before she continued, "Thank you for being honest with me. But where do you want to go from here? Because, I want to be clear. I won't be your secret anymore. I know I'm worth way more than that."

I let go of her hand and went over to the rose bush next to the bench. I picked one bright pink rose head and made a mental note to apologize to Serenity for picking from her mom's garden. I had noticed them earlier when I was smoking outside with Elijah. Under the moonlight, they looked darker and—I would argue—prettier. I walked back over to Mariposa and said, "I know you are, Mari. Which is why, if you'll let me, I would love to take you on a redo first date."

She started laughing as soon as she heard me say it, but not in a way that suggested she was making fun of the idea. She just seemed happy, and she had that big pearly white smile to prove it. "A redo date? What does that consist of? 'Cause if there's no food involved I might have to change my answer."

I rolled my eyes. "Don't worry, there'll be food and lots of fun. The week-long carnival starts on Monday, so how about that? We can go out to eat afterward so we don't feel sick on the rides."

"Alright, I'd like that. A redo date sounds like a plan."

"Good. I can't wait." I knew I had to win her trust back before anything else, but I was just happy she'd decided to give us another chance. We were going to be in different states in the fall, so who knew what our relationship would look like in three months? But even if it didn't work out with us, I'd rather look back at when I was nineteen and think about my amazing summer with my amazing girlfriend instead of wondering what could have been if I had just been honest.

Mariposa was right. There is no point in being in love if you let fear get in the way.

I had to stop being afraid, so I kissed her. This time, I didn't feel like I was kissing her just to hide the words I really wanted to say. I just wanted to kiss the girl I loved. The girl I was going on a date with soon. The girl I wanted to make my girlfriend. Later on, who knew? We were still so young.

That feeling was enough. We were enough. Everything felt perfect.

Bang!

The eerily familiar noise pierced through the air. Seconds later, it still lingered in the heat. We had grown up in shitty enough parts of the city to immediately recognize the sound. The worst part was that we both knew how close the shot sounded. Then we heard the screams and cries.

Too much ran through my mind. I didn't know what to do. Mari and I ran to look for our friends. We saw everybody pointing and screaming about the front yard, and no one was in sight. Not Raymond, Serenity, or Elijah. Not even Edwin, Valeria, or Diego.

Everything was so loud and so fast. Everything had changed with one second, one sound.

I grabbed for Mari's hand because she was screaming at everyone who would listen asking where Elijah was, but no one could give her a clear answer. I led her outside. As soon as we saw the mess, she broke down crying. I held her in my arms, but it was taking everything in me not to want to go down with her. I couldn't believe what I was seeing. Edwin was bleeding out, and everyone was around him. Three guys were running down the block. They were laughing and cheering. They were almost gone.

I searched the crowd for Raymond, who was crying on his knees while Serenity held him. Serenity had tears falling down her face but still managed to call out, "Mari, Jayden, please get over here and help me!"

Elijah and Diego were next to them already, trying to calm Raymond down. Mariposa ran straight to Elijah.

Edwin was on the ground, and Valeria was holding him as he bled onto her.

XV.

ELIJAH

"Rollarblades" - Dominic Fike

a single moment
a single decision
can change everything
it will drive us insane to think that we have any say
I don't mean to say that bad things are meant to be
but how could they not be?

- ESTHER HUESCAS

JUNE 2019

For a couple of minutes, I was in bliss thinking about how I no longer had to hide a huge part of myself from my best friends. I let myself daydream of walking hand in hand with Diego without a care as to who saw us.

"I'm finna fuck you up!" a mystery voice yelled from outside in the front yard.

The voice sent shivers down my spine. "Let's go," I said as I took Diego's hand and ran to the front.

When we got outside, I noticed that a lot of party guests were scattering down the block. I'd run away from a fight, too; I never saw a point in physically hurting someone else. It all seemed like a waste of time and for things that weren't worth it.

I saw Edwin and his friends celebrating because one of the guys from their rival gang was on the ground, holding onto his stomach and groaning in pain.

I saw Raymond standing near Edwin with his eyes wide. "Okay, let's all go home." The remaining upright gang members argued across the front yard.

No one listened to Raymond except for Serenity, who whispered something to him. A crease formed in between her eyebrows as she talked to him.

Raymond pleaded, "Come on, guys, you already did enough. We should all leave."

"See, those damn Disciples ain't got anything on us," Edwin screamed into the air. The rival guys were getting angrier and louder on the other side of the yard.

Instead of leaving it at that, one of Edwin's buddies got a little cocky. He went up to the guy on the ground and said, "Yo, fuck y'all Pulaski bitches. Y'all a bunch of pussies. Can't even take a punch. *Amor* to 18th. 'Til death, fool."

He spit on the rival disciple groaning on the ground.

As soon as his spit landed on the guy, the Disciples tackled Edwin's friend. All anyone could hear was their curses and groans.

They started beating him, hard. Edwin and the rest of the 18th gang jumped up and ran over to help their friend. They ended up getting the upper hand and were able to get the other guys off, but the whole thing got too messy. People were throwing punches everywhere, not caring where their fists landed as long as they connected with somebody.

I hadn't noticed that Diego had been holding my hand the entire time. He was shaking and holding me closer to him. Damn it, I was scared too, but I was trying really hard to look strong for him and for all my friends.

I followed Raymond's lead. He had started fighting Serenity's arms to go in and help. Diego held me back. "You can't do this, Elijah."

Serenity and Valeria were now both holding Raymond back. They all looked on as guys from both sides threw punches. Valeria didn't seem too worried, as if she'd seen this sort of thing many times before. I think her unfazed look initially kept me calm, but her expression soon became worried. She stopped whispering to Raymond and began to yell, "Raymond, make them stop! Stop!"

I looked back nervously from the chaos and saw that no one besides us was left. It was getting close to midnight, and the celebration was no longer what anyone expected it to be. I was worried that Serenity's birthday was turning out so badly. A day I thought I'd never forget—the moment I'd finally let myself be honest—had turned into a nightmare.

I felt Diego's hand in mine and was thankful that I had him next to me. I felt braver with him by my side. With all the chaos unfolding before us, I'd somehow completely forgotten that I hadn't come out to Serenity and Raymond yet. I knew I'd have to explain at a later time. The only thing that seemed important right then was breaking up the fight.

Grunts and groans of pain filled the air, along with Valeria pleading with Edwin to take her home. "Please, baby, let's leave. Edwin, stop it now! They get it!" Her pleas grew in urgency as the fighting continued.

Serenity tried to calm her down while Raymond kept saying, "Don't worry. He'll be fine."

Valeria looked up at him and said, "Yeah, well, Ray, you don't know either of us anymore."

"Okay, then I'm gonna go get him out."

Serenity still had her hands around him and tried to block him from going past her into the fight. "No, Raymond, please. I'm begging you. It's not worth it."

Raymond didn't stop to explain himself. He yelled back at Serenity, "I gotta do this!"

Raymond rushed Edwin and tried to talk to him, but he wasn't listening. Raymond grabbed Edwin's arm and yelled at him, "Let's leave, now!"

"I have to help them, Diego." I pulled away and was about to rush to Raymond and Edwin when everything started to really go to shit. Diego grabbed me and once again held me back.

Raymond and Edwin were arguing about leaving and had their backs turned away from the fight, which made them vulnerable. The Pulaski Disciples member who had been on the ground for the majority of the fight—the one who got spit on—stood up and pulled out a small, black handgun.

The guy from Edwin's gang who spit on him looked scared as fuck. He moved backward toward the rest of the 18th Street *Leyendas*. The gunman pointed the gun straight at Raymond with a stupid smirk on his face. "You bitch."

At first, I thought the bullet wasn't meant for anyone but the 18th member who had spit on him. I didn't realize that he really just wanted to see one of them shot—one of them or one of their friends.

Edwin screamed, "Get down!" to Raymond and threw himself in front of my friend.

Everything after that was a blur, but I remember the screams most vividly. Raymond and Valeria's pierced the air. I opened my mouth, but nothing came out.

The shot went directly into Edwin's left arm, and he collapsed immediately. He fell back on the grass, and his body thumped when it hit the ground. He screamed, "Fuck!" as he clutched his arm.

His voice rang through my ears long after he grew quiet. Valeria ran to his side as the Pulaski Disciples took off running. They laughed their way down the block.

Raymond was down on the ground, too. His eyes were wide in disbelief. Serenity was holding onto him and loudly crying into his shoulder. He couldn't stop looking at Edwin as tears streamed silently down his face and his body shook violently.

"Elijah!" Mariposa's voice came from behind me, and I immediately went to hug her. She was crying and through her wheezing, she kept saying, "Oh, my God! What if it'd been you who was hurt?"

All I could think was that I never wanted to leave her. She was and always would be my best friend, ever since the womb. Nothing could beat that.

Jayden and Diego rushed to Raymond and managed to pull him and Serenity away from Edwin. The five of us stood together and looked in disbelief at Edwin bleeding. Serenity called 911 and was on the phone with them explaining the situation. We hugged Raymond, who was quietly sobbing and muttering, "I'm sorry."

The ambulance came, and Valeria went with Edwin to the hospital. The police sirens tried to drown out our cries, but surprisingly, they were failing.

The inside of Serenity's house was the skeleton of a party. Red solo cups covered the floor; people had dropped them as they left in a hurry. I convinced Diego to go home and that I would be fine with the others. I kissed him goodnight and promised to let him know when I got home. Our parents eventually got to Serenity's house.

By the time the police came, the Pulaski Disciples were long gone. The police took our statements on the incident, but it was obvious they were just asking the questions to fill out the forms. They didn't seem to care once they heard it was gang related. They only seemed to see that Edwin was brown, he was in a gang, and we were in a poor, black neighborhood in the southside of Chicago. It pissed me off. It always had.

They were satisfied knowing he was on his way to the hospital and would receive help there. For them and for the system, we were just another statistic. So, no, the police didn't do enough. They never do enough for people like us.

XVI.

VALERIA

"Another Lifetime" - Nao

what do I do now
that you're changing and becoming someone I no longer recognize
what do I do now
that you're leaving me
what do I live off of now
when you were my **only** breath of fresh air
for so long.

- ESTHER HUESCAS

JUNE 2019

"Edwin! You gonna be alright."

That's all I kept saying. As I watched the only man I'd ever loved bleed onto me, our friends tried to figure out whether or not to wait with me until the police came. I knew they wouldn't stay. Although I believed they did care for him, the fear of getting arrested was bigger than anything else.

"Valeria, I'm so sorry," Edwin muttered through gasping breaths. Pain spread across his face.

Raymond and his friends' voices surrounded us, but, in that moment, Edwin was the only one I could hear or see.

As I looked into his eyes, the day we first met flashed through my mind.

I was excited to make the move from Humboldt Park to Little Village. In my old home, I lived with my Venezuelan mother and Puerto Rican father in a small apartment across from the park. When I was six, I was told to pack my things because we were moving to a real house.

When I learned that our new house had a backyard, I was excited to play with my parents. I also quickly learned that my uncle had bought the house and his eight boys would be living there as well. All the boys were older than me, and they crushed my dreams of having my own room.

I met Edwin the week I moved in, and we quickly became inseparable. I loved hanging out with him because he never made me feel bad about not wanting to go home. He didn't judge me when we were ten and I told him I didn't like my cousins because they tried to touch me at night. He didn't stop being my friend when we were twelve and I would cry to him about the body parts they showed me.

As our friends were getting ready to leave, I wondered whether or not they were worth calling family. I asked myself, "*Who leaves family alone when they're hurt?*" They tried to convince me to go with them by pulling me from the ground, but I twisted and fought back against their grip. I fell back down hard and hit my knees. "I love you. I'm not leaving you!" I screamed to Edwin. They gave up on me and left.

At fifteen, I turned all that pain about my family into anger. I was angry, so I started hanging out with older guys whose ages I sometimes hid from even Edwin. Some were seventeen and eighteen, but others were twenty-one and twenty-two. I didn't care about them. The only man I wanted in my life was Edwin. I lost my virginity to him because I knew that he wouldn't hurt me. Yet, I didn't want to mess things up by fooling around with him all the time.

So, we stopped. Instead, after every date, I'd go to Edwin's room. I'd share with him the money and gifts the men would buy for me. Older men with money to spare were so generous, simply because they thought I was pretty. They also got me into weed after a while, but despite all my adventures, I still did really well in school.

I thought back at how we met Raymond at sixteen. I'd immediately thought he was so fine. I loved the way he dressed, specifically, how he always looked and acted presentable. I also loved that he wasn't from the hood. I loved that he went to church with his perfect family every Sunday. But I didn't love *him*. So, unlike with Edwin, I didn't mind messing things up by fooling around.

I looked down at my love's shirt, which was covered with my tears. I barely noticed how they didn't seem to want to stop. We heard the sounds of sirens coming down the block. I realized our friends had left right on time.

Edwin was my rock, and I never judged him when he said he wanted to join the 18th Street *Leyendas*, even after Raymond stopped being friends with us because of it. Edwin had never judged me, so I knew I could never judge him. I'd be lying to myself if I didn't admit part of me wished he hadn't joined. I knew he was putting himself in danger. Still, even when he dropped out of school, he'd drop me off and pick me up every single day, at first on the train and then later in his car.

I was terrified by seeing what gang lifestyle had led us to: a random party on a Friday night, covered in Edwin's blood. I thought back to the day we had promised each other forever.

The paramedics ran from the ambulance to where I was with Edwin. They began to work on him, and I tried my hardest to not let go of his hand.

When we were seventeen, another typical summer night ended up being different. We talked about our futures, and Edwin was envisioning his restaurant named *La Casita.* He said he wanted us to own the restaurant together, and he'd be the head chef. Edwin said that was the perfect name because it would be a place where everyone could find a little home.

Apart from *La Casita,* I wanted to get my degree and become a social worker. I dreamed of being able to help children so they'd never have to deal with the messed-up stuff I went through. I wanted to help them before they turned to gangs and drugs. When we realized we saw each other in our own futures, we kissed. I kissed Edwin for the first time in two years that night, but I didn't fear that I'd mess things up with him this time around. I was sure that I loved him, and he loved me. That's exactly what we told each other. We promised each other that night to always end the night together.

I climbed onto the back of the ambulance and held Edwin's hand. I couldn't leave him there. I never would. I promised him all my nights, and I had no intention of breaking that promise. The paramedic hopped in the back with us and closed the door behind her. We were finally on route to the hospital.

XVII.

RAYMOND

"Nuestro Planeta" - Kali Uchis ft. Reykon

the saying goes
if you love someone let them go
if they come back
it was meant to be
if they don't
they were never yours.
the saying forgets that this can't always be the case
they sometimes come back when they shouldn't
just to make sure you've learned your lesson.
yet here we are together
it's clear to me now you still haven't learned.

\- ESTHER HUESCAS

JUNE 2019

I didn't know how it would feel to face death until I looked down the barrel of the gun. I knew I wasn't safe from gun violence just by living in the Northside and being in college; I knew more than anything that as a Black man in Chicago, there was nothing I could do to escape that risk. Which was exactly why I stopped being friends with Edwin and Valeria.

My heart was racing as I saw Edwin hurt on the ground. I couldn't believe he had jumped in front of me to save me. I hadn't seen him in years, and he did it without hesitation. As soon as the shot went off, Edwin fell to the ground. I followed and fell to my knees. Serenity was crying next me as she held me. I knew she was talking to me, but I wasn't processing her words. All the screams coming from everyone sounded like a buzz. All I could see was Edwin.

I realized as the ambulance pulled up and took Edwin that I still felt guilty. I had been feeling guilty for the last three years. I blamed myself for having been distracted with Valeria the summer he got jumped in. I blamed Valeria for not stopping him.

I didn't know what I would've done with myself if the shot had been worse. I didn't even want to let myself wonder what I would've done if he'd died that night. He didn't; that's ultimately all that mattered. A lot of things seemed clearer as Valeria and Edwin left in the ambulance.

What broke my heart more than any of my confusion and self-blame was seeing Serenity cry. She wasn't letting me leave her side and held me as I cried. I didn't know what to do about a lot of things, but I did know I never wanted to not be able to call her mine. I realized tragedy has a way of showing us what's important in life.

Valeria and Edwin had each other, and their relationship worked for them. That's what I had to remember. Valeria was strong, and I knew she'd get through it. I could only hope that seeing Edwin like that would wake something up inside her and that the mere thought of being in that situation again would scare her for good. I couldn't imagine seeing the person she was in love with—her best friend for fourteen years—bleeding in her arms.

It wasn't my job or responsibility anymore to worry if they bettered their lives. My responsibility was to make sure Serenity was good and happy. Tonight, I'd failed her as her boyfriend, but more importantly, as her best friend.

I knew I'd have to make it up to her. I didn't want to be the reason why she cried ever again. I blamed myself for inviting them to her birthday party.

I held her tightly in a bear hug. "Serenity, I'm so sorry."

She rubbed my back and held on to me. "I know, Raymond. I know."

I'd gone to church on Sunday mornings ever since I could remember. Like clockwork, I'd get up and get dressed in my Sunday best. Praying at night before I went to sleep had therefore become second nature.

My thoughts that night to God were:

"I want to be a better man. I want to be a better friend. More than anything, I need to be a better man for Serenity. I need to be the type of man who deserves a woman like her. God, I hope you guide Edwin and Valeria in a better direction, but I hope you won't be upset to hear that I can no longer be there to make sure that happens. I have no hate in my heart for either of them. I know that despite them having brought violence into Serenity's home, they aren't bad people. I urge you to not to let me mess things up with Serenity. I love her."

* * *

THE AFTERMATH

The following days we all went to Mariposa and Elijah's house like the good old days. We spent as much time together as possible, so we took fewer hours at work. Life seemed so short and way too unpredictable. We promised each other that we'd spend the summer together as much as possible before going off to different parts of the country in the fall.

I'd promised Serenity a date, and that is exactly what I did.

The Wednesday after the party, I picked her up to take her to the beach. As I pulled up, I couldn't help but notice that I saw her house in a different light now. Serenity had mowed the lawn, which hid what had happened just a few days before.

She came out of the house with a pair of blue jean shorts and a pink tank top on. She looked so perfect in the most carefree way possible. Seeing her there brought back the same feeling I felt when I picked her up for our first date, almost three years before. All I felt were butterflies.

I got out to open the door, which made me remember how beautiful Chicago was in the summertime. The sun seemed to smile down on us.

"Hey, beautiful," I said as I hugged her.

She pulled back and kissed me. "Hey, cutie."

I thought back to how we'd spent Sunday night on the phone with each other for hours. I'd wanted to spend the day with my family since every other day I'd spent with my friends, but I knew I needed to talk to her alone. We ended up on the phone crying to each other as I explained to her that I never meant to hurt her.

I knew she'd never make me feel bad about how everything went down, but it didn't mean I didn't do anything wrong.

After Serenity kissed me, she asked, "Raymond, how're you feeling?"

I turned on the radio. "Better, I think. How about you?" I noticed she was wearing her ring, and it looked better on her than it had in the box. I let myself imagine a day when I could turn that promise ring into an engagement ring and then add a wedding band. I liked the idea of that.

"I feel a lot better. Have you heard from Edwin or Valeria yet?"

"Yeah, I talked to Edwin last night. He said he's gonna be in the hospital for a while, but he should be all right."

I didn't tell Serenity that when I got on the call and heard his voice, I was ready to curse him out. I wanted to yell at him for bringing so much danger into our lives, but I chose not to. I felt like it would be better to just let things be the way they were. I didn't want to worry Serenity, either. I reached for her hand on her lap and held it as I drove.

"I'm glad. So, what's the plan today? I see a picnic basket."

We drove up north on Lake Shore to get to North Avenue Beach. We passed downtown and soon the skyscrapers turned into condo buildings. The lake shined bright, and the beaches were already packed. "We're going to watch the sunset from the beach and eat some snacks. Does that sound all right?"

She immediately smiled at me with all her pearly white teeth. "Sounds perfect."

We finally found parking after what seemed like forever. I had the picnic basket and blanket in one hand and her hand in the other. The sun was slowly going down, and the sky was painted in shades of orange, pink, and purple. I hadn't brought much to eat, just some chips and juice. I knew we'd get some food on the way back.

Despite being around so many other people, we still felt like we were in our own bubble filled with love—just two people trying to better themselves. We spent the entire time talking about everything and anything. I felt like I was getting to know her all over again. I was angry at myself for ever taking her for granted.

I knew that moment was my definition of perfection as I sprawled next to her on the blanket looking up at the sky and seeing the clouds disappear into the night. I felt at peace and grateful to be with her. Grateful to be alive.

EPILOGUE

XVIII.

MARIPOSA

"Moon River" - Frank Ocean

how do you say goodbye to something you don't want
to end?
you don't.
you choose to make it timeless instead.

- ESTHER HUESCAS

NOVEMBER 2019

I landed on Saturday morning from UCLA, and Jayden came to pick me up at O'Hare. Friendsgiving was on Wednesday, and we'd hung out almost every day up to then. I missed them all, especially Elijah. I would've never admitted it to him, but I was missing our twin bonding time.

Thanksgiving that year was a lot more important for everyone than it had been before. We were all now in college and had started to figure out what we wanted to study. In some ways, all of our lives had changed in the past months.

That's why we'd decided to have a Friendsgiving get-together at our house. It made the most sense to us to have it the night before Thanksgiving so that we could spend a couple hours of the actual holiday together, too.

Jayden came over to our house at almost two in the afternoon, just as Elijah came down the stairs into the kitchen with huge bedhead, groaning and looking for food. Our parents had gone to work early and wouldn't be home until really late because they said they wanted to give the five of us our space. So, after work, they'd planned to visit my aunt and her family in the suburbs.

I was in front of the kitchen island when I noticed Elijah. "Good morning, sleepyhead," I said as I proudly pointed at the uncooked but fully prepared turkey in front of me.

Elijah's eyes widened. "Bruh, Mari, how you up already cooking?"

I had started getting the turkey ready when my parents left since I knew that it would take the longest. Elijah and I were in charge of the main course because we were the hosts and it would be a lot for someone else to bring a whole turkey. I loved to cook, so I didn't mind having the most difficult dish. Elijah's contribution to the meal was more in spirit. He'd made the executive decision to make his job to eat. What a bum.

Jayden came in behind Elijah and laughed. "Yeah, Mari, you're crazy." He came up to me and kissed me on the cheek. "But I love it."

Elijah quickly covered his eyes and looked away. "Ew, please stop. I don't want to see that. I liked it better when I could pretend y'all weren't dating." Wide awake now, he dramatically said, "Ugh, the good old days."

I couldn't help but laugh because he and Diego were more guilty of PDA than we were. I didn't think we were that cringey.

"Hey, babe," I said to Jayden and made kissing noises just to annoy Elijah further.

"Please stop, you both are making my eyes burn."

The three of us started laughing, and Elijah left up the stairs after claiming he'd be back in five minutes.

Diego and Elijah had spent the entire summer going out. Elijah came out to our parents as gay shortly after the shooting. He told me the night before he talked to them about how even though he was terrified, he didn't want to hide that part of himself from them anymore. He confessed to me that he felt life was so uncertain after the shooting.

Elijah had invited Diego for Friendsgiving, too, but he was spending the week on vacation with his family so he couldn't come. Since Diego went to UIC and Elijah went to Northwestern, their relationship had been going great. Elijah would call me and tell me about the cute dates they had over the weekend and how they'd meet up during the week to study. Elijah had also gotten really involved in bringing college prep resources and support to poor black and brown neighborhoods in Chicago. He'd started an initiative at Northwestern and was working with the rest of us to implement the program in our schools.

I knew Elijah too well. He didn't come back down until Serenity and Raymond arrived.

I put the turkey in the oven and left it to cook for the next three hours. I then put the sweet potatoes and mashed potatoes that Jayden had made in the fridge. I decided I wouldn't warm them up until the turkey was closer to being done. I'd just finished cleaning up when Jayden asked, "Guess what?"

He had the silliest smile on his face. I just wanted to grab his face and kiss him. I asked, "What?"

He held up a black plastic bag and said, "I bought the wine you been wanting to try. It was pretty cheap. I got them both for twenty dollars."

"Perfect! Now we can act classy and have some wine with dinner." Jayden was goofy and sweet. I wondered how I got this lucky. I grabbed two glasses from the cupboard and opened one of the wine bottles. I served us both and as I gave him his glass, I said, "But one before dinner won't hurt, either."

He laughed. "You right. You know it's not too chilly outside, especially in the sun." He extended his hand so I could grab it and asked, "Will you join me on your balcony?"

"Yes, of course." I grabbed his hand and let him lead me to my bedroom where there was a small balcony. Before I went out, I grabbed a sweater from my closet for the breeze.

I had some floor pillows scattered on the balcony, and we arranged them so we could sit next to each other. The sun hit us perfectly from up there and offered relief from the cool breeze as it hit my face. I let my head rest on Jayden's shoulder after taking a sip of the wine, which honestly tasted pretty good. From where we were sitting, we could see the entire busy avenue in front of us. People were busy shopping for Thanksgiving, and kids were running around the sidewalk. Older kids rode their bikes down the street. Chicago was alive.

We were so close together that I could smell the smokiness of his cologne. "It's been like two-and-a-half years since we met, Jayden. Isn't that crazy?"

He looked so perfect. I thought back to all the amazing memories I'd made with him in the last few years, specifically during the past summer. We ended up having our re-do first date at a small music and food festival in Logan Square on Logan Boulevard. We got there pretty early in the afternoon and got full from free samples really quickly. We listened to some small local Chicago artists who put on some really good sets. Later in the afternoon, we rented some divvy bikes and took them to watch the sunset on North Avenue Beach.

It was perfect, and I spent the entire time daydreaming about a future in which we were together—a future where our own pasts and our parents' vices couldn't reach us.

The rest of the summer was just as magical. We kept going on dates, and I'd be lying if I didn't admit that I'd fallen in love with him all over again. He'd gotten a pretty dark tan over the summer that somehow made his smile and eyes seem brighter. The difference with the magic of that summer versus the one before was that we were no longer a secret. He was my boyfriend, I was his girlfriend, and we reintroduced each other to our families like that.

My mother had tried to convince me that she knew Jayden was in love with me before I even knew. She called it "mother's intuition." I just laughed her away and rolled my eyes, but part of me wanted to believe her. My father tried the tough guy approach and grilled Jayden for a good thirty minutes, but he eventually gave it up. He said that if he had to deal with anyone dating his only daughter, he was happy it was Jayden.

At the end of the summer, we said we'd try a long-distance relationship. Chicago and Los Angeles are 2,015 miles apart. The first couple of weeks were the hardest because it was unclear how much communication was too much. I had to fight my urge to want to know what he was doing all the time or get jealous if we went a day without talking. I honestly think I was just lonely. Once I started getting closer to my roommate, Daniela, and made more friends in class and at parties, I started to let go. I didn't let go of loving Jayden, but I just wasn't so stuck on needing to talk to him every day. This Thanksgiving break was the first time we'd seen each other since I left in September.

He kissed my hand softly and with his big smile, he said, "Yeah, it's been a wild time, huh?"

I beamed as I thought back at how it felt when he kissed me for the first. All the butterflies. "Do you think your story has changed?"

Jayden's eyebrows furrowed, and he turned to face me. He asked, "My story?"

"Yeah. The first question I ever asked you was what your story was. Could you have guessed we'd end up here?" As I looked at him, I realized that he still gave me those damn butterflies.

"Yeah, it's definitely changed. I wasn't the man I hoped to be back then. I'm still tryna be better, you know."

"Yeah, I feel that. I'm tryna better myself, too." The sun had been setting really early, and today was no exception. As we sat there, the sky turned a beautiful periwinkle. The bright orange sun slowly disappeared.

Several moments passed where we didn't talk, and the only thing you could hear in the air was the car horns of angry Chicagoans stuck in traffic.

"Mariposa? Jayden? Y'all up there?" Serenity yelled from my front yard, holding bags filled with Friendsgiving dishes. She stood next to Raymond, who looked like he'd gotten stuck carrying the heavy pans and a bouquet of tulips.

Edwin's shooting had brought Raymond and Serenity closer together. She had told me how much more seriously she'd taken their relationship since her birthday. They were almost going to stay in New York for break because the flights were too expensive. Their apartment already costed them both a lot of hours at their minimum-wage jobs. Fortunately, Raymond's parents came through and surprised them with flights once they heard how much they wanted to come back home.

Their apartment in New York City was small but really pretty. It was in a quiet neighborhood in between Columbia and NYU. It was a studio apartment, and I remembered being worried that it wouldn't give them enough space. Yet, for only being one room, it was kind of spacious. They had one large desk that they shared. They told us when they gave us the virtual tour in the beginning of fall that it never felt small to them. Serenity had the time of her life decorating it. We spent hours on the phone talking about room decor we'd seen on Pinterest.

Serenity and I still talked almost every week on the phone. At first, we had agreed to a set time every Sunday afternoon, but sometimes it wouldn't work out with our schedules. We ended up missing a couple weeks, but whenever we did talk, it felt as if we were in my dorm room together.

We'd call and tell each other about our classes and complain about our upcoming exams and papers. We'd catch each other up on gossip about the friends we'd made. Even if it didn't make much sense to each other, we'd listen. We'd sometimes get names mixed up when asking for follow ups on stories about friends or parties, but it was fun. During low points when I would be in my room feeling homesick, Facetiming Serenity and Raymond would lift my mood instantly.

I smiled at the sight of them. I yelled back, "Yep, it's us. We'll come down."

Elijah opened the front door for them as I said that and he teased, "You see what I'm dealing with here?" He pointed at us, and I swear I heard him roll his eyes as he said it.

"Shut up, Elijah!" I yelled back.

Raymond laughed. "Let them be, man, they're still in the honeymoon stage. We'll see y'all down here soon!"

With that, they went inside the house. I turned to Jayden who was sitting there smiling at me, making me nervous as he could always do so well. "We should probably go down now."

"Yeah, but first—" He finished his sentence by softly grabbing my face and kissing me.

I was happy. That was all I wanted. Despite everything that had happened, we were happy.

Jayden held my hand. "About my story. . . it changed the second I met you. I'm really happy it did too, 'cause the feeling I get when I'm with you, Mari. . . that's what I call love now."

"Me, too," I said as those butterflies kept on fluttering.

THE END

ACKNOWLEDGMENTS

I would like to start off by first and foremost thanking my family. Ma, Pa, and Benji; you three have always been my biggest supporters. I know this would not have been possible without your love and support throughout all my endeavors. The support I have felt from my entire family has been unbelievable.

I do not know who I would be if it wasn't for the friendships that I have gained throughout the years. I remember speaking to my friends in the Summer of 2019 about my wild dream of writing this book. I have been writing my entire life; I have filled out more journals and diaries than I care to admit. Thank you to my friends since high school: Alison, Emilia, Gillianna, Kimberly, Nneoma, and Zainab.

I could have never imagined I would be in a position to be thanking people for helping me complete this milestone, especially at nineteen. *What We Call Love* started as a dream I didn't dare say out loud. Thanks to the encouragement of my writing skills from my high school English teacher and mentor, Timothy Jung, I was able to find the courage to admit that writing a novel was a goal of mine.

I would like to say a huge thank you to Eric Koester and everyone at New Degree Press. Thank you for believing in me the second I shared my idea. Specifically, I would like to thank Jemiscoe Chambers-Black, Carol McKibben, and Brian Bies. Your advice and suggestions made the book what it is now.

Finally, I would like to thank everyone who allowed me to interview them and get to know their opinions on love, relationships, and social justice issues. To everyone who pre-ordered my eBook, paper book, or both to make publishing possible, I am eternally grateful for you all.

Thank you to everyone I interviewed:

Ngozi Amadikwu
Alex Chavez
Carlos Gallegos
Gillianna Hernandez
Hajra Lat
Nina Oforji
Daniel Soto
Jose Vasquez
Nestor J. Barrera
Rafael Diaz
Adrian Garces
Sarah Kamal
Abdi Lawrence
Daviana Soberanis
Alison Tatchoum

Thank you to everyone who pre-ordered my book:

Adedoyin Akisanya
Ngozi Amadikwu
Maame Boateng
Elizabeth Buergo
Perla Casillas
Federico Ceja
Emilia Chojnacki
Jayson Coy
Joel Itzcoatl Martinez Coss
Adrian Garces
Norma Esther Coss Garcia
Grace Geevarghese
Erin Goldman
Kimberly Grabiec
Phyllis Hencke
Gillianna Hernandez
Paloma Hernandez
Benjamin Huescas
Ricardo Huescas
Timothy Jung
Eric Koester
Kathleen Kuziel
Guy Lohoua
Sandra M Morad
Humayra A. Munshi
Daniel Novaes
Mayda Nunez
Jesús Antonio Ochoa
Sara Coss de Ochoa
Kiara Aldana
Sasha Aristizabal
Seth Bos
Janine Castellanos
Monsetrratt Castillo
Alex Chavez
Joselyn Cordero
Anthony Coss
Arianna Fritz
Carlos Gallegos
Sahira Coss Garcia
David Golden
Jessica Gomez
Edina Hadzic
Kelly Herlihy
Jaredth Hernandez
Hannah Horvath
Maria Huescas
Terrell James
Alvin Kang
Genevieve Kosciolek
Mark Lawrence
Brittney Mensah
Martha Mulligan
Inyoung Nah
Areli Nunez
Daniella Ochoa
Pablo Ochoa
Nina Oforji

Osazee Osaghae

Kiran Panesar

Max Powell

Tum Promlee

Miguel Rascon

KC Rivera

Aidan Robertson

Arturo Romero

Scott Rovner

Ewa Sak

Daviana Soberanis

Natan Spear

Melissa Suarez

Alison Tatchoum

Jennifer Tegegne

Gabriel M.Tejeda

Joan Tepavchevich

Vicente Torres

Zainab Umardeen

Jake Watson

Erick Vasquez

Jose Vazquez

Rosa Vega

Alina Yamin

CPSIA information can be obtained
at www.ICGtesting.com
Printed in the USA
FSHW021433271220